Blaze

Also by Robert Somerlott
The Flamingos
The Inquisitor's House
Here, Mr. Splitfoot

Blaze

Robert Somerlott

The Viking Press   New York

For Tom Brock Scott
and for Viking, Margarita, and Destry.

First published in 1981 by The Viking Press
625 Madison Avenue, New York, N.Y. 10022
Published simultaneously in Canada by
Penguin Books Canada Limited

LIBRARY OF CONGRESS CATALOGING IN PUBLICATION DATA
Somerlott, Robert.
Blaze.
I. Title.
PZ4.S6916Bl   [PS3569.06516]   813′.54   80-17158
ISBN 0-670-17368-1

Printed in the United States of America
Set in Garamond

Blaze

One

In just a few miles the road had plunged from the mountains into the Mojave Desert, and the truck was in barren, hostile country offering neither water nor shelter when the hitchhiker began to suspect that the old man driving the vehicle was demented. By that time nothing could be done about it.

The hitchhiker, a college student, had felt doubtful when he accepted a ride in the cab of this rattletrap camper; he had realized that both the vehicle and its driver were odd, but the notion that the lean but muscular old man might be a little crazy had not crossed his mind.

He had been stranded near a crossroads hamlet, the last mountain village on the northwestern rim of the Mojave Desert. Slowly the heat of the afternoon had risen, and although his backpack was not heavy, it became uncomfortably warm. Taking it off, he sought refuge in the speckled shade of a mesquite tree, and had almost despaired of ever encountering traffic on this road when he heard in the distance an angry grinding of a motor and three sharp backfires. Then the vehicle itself came into view, rounding a long curve, an ancient Ford pickup truck that had been converted into an oversize camper by the addition of plywood walls and a tin roof, an awkward, boxy construction that jutted out behind both sides of the cab and loomed high above it.

The hitchhiker put on an ingratiating grin, waved his thumb vigorously, and to his relief the truck slowed, the backfiring diminished, and the vehicle came to a halt a few yards beyond him. He ran to the passenger door, but was baffled when he found the handle was missing. The van, he noticed, had once been painted in flamboyant pinks, reds, and yellows, but the colors were now faded and peeling. There was a pale shape of some huge insect and a name had been neatly stenciled on the side: The Green Hornet.

The door, opened from the inside, swung out suddenly, narrowly missing the hitchhiker, who found a fierce-looking old man leaning across the seat, examining him. Sharp blue eyes raked the hitchhiker, eyes set in a face as weathered, wrinkled, and tanned as the bark of a live oak tree. His thick hair and short-cropped pointed beard were iron gray except for two silver streaks at his temples. On the back of his head, cocked at a jaunty angle, he wore a blue cap with a sun vizor that made him look like a sea captain.

"Need a ride?" asked the old man gruffly.

"Yes, thanks," said the hitchhiker. Then he added, "Yes, *sir*," a form of address he had not used since he ceased being afraid of his father. He did not know why he used it now, but something in that wintery blue-eyed gaze made him feel he was standing for a military inspection, and the old man seemed to wear invisible epaulets on the shoulders of his embroidered Mexican shirt.

The hitchhiker stepped forward, then hesitated, afraid of being stranded again in an unlikely place. "Where you bound, sir?"

"East," came the noncommittal reply.

"I mean are you crossing the desert?"

"Such is my hope and intention." The old man arched a pessimistic eyebrow. His brows were bristly and they combined with the beard and the hollows of his cheeks and temples to give him the look of a well-barbered Viking. "God willing, we shall be delivered from the wastes of California and reach the promised land."

A joke? Again the hitchhiker hesitated, not because the old man might be a religious fanatic, but because he feared being recruited as a tire changer or emergency mechanic. Still, this might be his last chance for a ride today.

Nodding, he put his backpack on the floor of the cab and climbed in. When he leaned to shut the door, a broken seat spring stabbed his right buttock. *"Ouch!"* he cried. It was an omen.

The old man, busy fumbling with wires under the dashboard, paid no attention. When he touched two wires together, the motor roared to life, a roar that quickly subsided to whines, coughs, and grindings. The clutch, being released, emitted an ear-splitting screech, and the Green Hornet gave a lurch, then limped forward.

The glass had been removed from the rear window of the cab and replaced with a chain-link mesh of steel set in a wooden frame. The screened opening was not large, a little more than a foot wide and half as high, but looking over his shoulder, the hitchhiker had an impression of the dark interior of the van. He made out the shape of a large wooden box—no, not a box, he decided, a big cage with wooden sides and a door made of a metal grating. Twisting in his seat, he determined that an identical cage stood next to this one. What could be imprisoned in these? Animals for a zoo? Was the old man connected with a circus? A medicine show? Just then from the rear came a savage snarling, followed by bangs and crashes as some animal hurled itself at the door of an unseen cage.

A large and powerful dog seemed the animal most likely to make such noises. But why, thought the hitchhiker, would anyone be driving around the country with a truck full of cages for *dogs*? It made no sense.

The old man appeared oblivious. Lost in contemplation, he gazed narrow-eyed at the road. He sat erect, as though in a saddle instead of a seat, his calloused hands gripping opposite sides of the steering wheel as if it were the invisible reins of a horse expected to buck at any moment.

When the snarling reached a pitch of frenzy, the hitchhiker asked loudly, "A wolf?"

"What?"

"That big animal back there. Is it a wolf?"

"Good Lord, no!" said the old man, then added sternly, "Wolves, young fellow, are not big animals except in the north. Wolves of this region wouldn't be much bigger than a malamute or a sammy."

And what's a malamute? thought the hitchhiker. Some

kind of elephant? And who's Sammy? But he said, "Not a wolf."

"I am returning a dangerous juvenile delinquent to his original home, you might say. It's not a job I wanted or expected."

It was then that the hitchhiker began to wonder if the old man might be a little crazy.

The sounds of attack subsided, and even the motor quieted on the long downgrade into the desert. They rode without speaking, and some dark mood had settled on the old man. Several times he shook his head, giving a little sigh that was both protest and futility. He seemed unaware of the hitchhiker, who leaned back in the seat and tried to doze, lulled by the monotonous chugging of the motor and by the enervating warmth of the afternoon.

His eyelids remained closed for some minutes, he drifted into sleep, then slowly awakened. Drowsily, he half opened his eyes and found himself looking into the rearview mirror above the windshield. Jiggled by the motion of the truck, it had come to rest in such a way that the hitchhiker saw a reflection of the mesh-covered window, a dark rectangle, and, suddenly, the face of a child, a small boy, who gazed silently through the wire into the cab. The hitchhiker had an impression of a fall of thick dark hair, pale cheeks, and large gray eyes that seemed strangely luminous, catching light in the shadows behind the mesh. To the hitchhiker's sleep-filled eyes, it was a wavering and uncertain picture like an image in shimmering water.

The impression dissolved, the features withdrawing or fading into dimness, and the hitchhiker sat up, blinking, startled awake, feeling that what he had just seen was not part of a dream, yet there was a curious unreality about the strange and unexpected appearance of the watching child.

He turned his head and tried to peer through the mesh, but the boy had vanished.

The driver had said he was transporting a juvenile delinquent. This little boy? Perhaps the van was a mobile prison, and the old man a tracker of runaway children. The word *tracker* made him think of the snarling animal, and he wondered if it might be a bloodhound. In his mind he had no picture of a bloodhound, but it was a dreadful name suggesting a creature that pursued you by the very scent of your blood—for which it thirsted. This thought, and the thought of children locked in the van's cages, made the hitchhiker very uneasy.

The old man began to sing, and his voice, curt and crusty when he spoke, rose with surprising warmth.

"O'er the measureless range, where seldom change
The swart gray plains, so weird and strange.
Treeless and streamless, yet wondrous still . . ."

He was not singing to himself or to his companion in the cab. With his head slightly turned and tilted toward the wire mesh, he appeared to be singing to the rear of the vehicle, to the van that imprisoned the boy and the animal.

He finished the song, and still directing his voice over his shoulder, he said, "Only a few miles more, boy, and we'll be at the Arizona line. If there's anything worse for us than red mange, it's been the state of California. We'll be glad to be out of it, won't we, boy?"

The old man, noticing the dubious expression on the hitchhiker's face, said, "They all like to be talked to, it's part of socializing them. You talk or you sing. Maybe I'm getting through to that fellow back there." He gestured toward the rear of the van with his thumb. "Unless he's just too far gone—turned crazy from mistreatment." The old man's fist suddenly banged the steering wheel with startling force. "People! Most of 'em aren't fit to be called animals, much less humans. Or should it be the other way around?"

Covertly the hitchhiker edged a little farther from the driver and a little closer to the door on the passenger side. The silence that followed the outburst seemed fraught with dangerous possibilities, the old man's rage was deep and bitter, and the hitchhiker tried to ease the situation with a light remark. "That's a good-looking boy you've got back there."

"Good-looking?" It was a snort. "In my life—and, believe me, I am long on years, breeds, and examples—I've seen few of God's creatures that were so beautiful. That's the pity of it. Why he's sheer fire! Blaze! Fire and steel and quicksilver. A panther could envy the way he moves . . . But how do you know what he looks like? You haven't seen him."

"I had a glimpse of him a few minutes ago—when he looked through the window."

"Looked through the—?" The old man cast a doubtful glance at the hitchhiker. "What the devil are you talking about?"

"The little boy who's in the van. I saw him in the mirror. I was just waking up and—"

"Well, young fellow, since you don't appear to be drinking, I conclude you've been dreaming. There's nobody there but Blaze, thank the Lord."

"Sure. Dreaming," said the hitchhiker uncertainly, and managed a weak smile, wondering if they would ever come to the main highway. An instant melodrama formed in his mind: the old man was a kidnapper, the child had been confined in a cage but had escaped, and now the old man denied his presence. He decided to treat the old man with great caution.

They were well into the Mojave now, and the landscape on all sides was a panorama of harshness and hostility. Dark mesas walled off the sky, their shale and sandstone smoldering in the sun. No creature, the hitchhiker thought, could survive long among these unyielding rocks.

It was late spring and the desert bloomed, the bitterbrush was tipped with yellow, scorpion weed displayed a delicate lavender that belied its sinister name, and wherever a little earth covered the rock floor orange flowers of ocotillo struggled to seize the ground from the sky-blue lupine, whose blossoms mixed with the ocotillo like two converging armies.

But the flowers could not disguise the gaunt land, a place of struggle so fierce that even the plants were spiked, armored, and bristling. Near the highway the bodies of two stripped automobiles, wrecked long ago, rusted in the afternoon sun. A little farther on stood the ruins of a burned-out cabin, a memorial to someone's false hope, its crumbling brick chimney as blackened as the natural-rock stovepipes of the desert surrounding this desolate spot. A set of charred bedsprings still leaned against the chimney, skeletal.

The old man lifted his voice above the rasping motor, half speaking, half singing. ". . . In the midst of the valley which was full of bones . . . there were very many in the open valley and they were very dry. . . . Our bones are dried and our hope is lost." He sighed, and said quietly to the hitchhiker, or perhaps to himself, "The words don't much matter. It's the sound of your voice that means something. It has to be strong and caring. And always, above everything else, it has to sound like love. . . ."

Blaze crouched in the deep shadows on the floor of the cage, disturbed, wary, and as alert as a switchblade.

He was only ten months old, but he already had the lithe, powerful body of an adult German Shepherd Dog, though his young muscles were not yet fully hardened and the rugged frame, built for tireless running, had not filled out. Nor had he yet acquired the weight that would give him even greater force—he was now a little less than eighty pounds, and his heavy bones were made to carry more than ninety.

His magnificent body had outdistanced his brain. His mind, his emotions, remained confused and unformed. Blaze had as yet no notion of his place in the world or of any purpose in his life; he was familiar with abuse, but had no experience of kindness, and as his strength had grown, so had his anger.

He was a dog that had never played. Never had he run

free across a meadow, or prowled the woods, or even known the companionship of a human or of his own kind.

Only vague promptings of instinct, the collective experience of generations, kept him from savagery; he was undeveloped except as a machine superbly designed for attack and destruction, a living weapon, but a weapon without guidance or control. And unlike a machine or a weapon, Blaze had felt pain and longing.

Now he peered through the steel grating of the door into the darkness of the van. To his sensitive eyes it was not darkness, but what a man would have called twilight. At times he moved his head slightly from side to side, for his vision was sharper when he moved, just as he saw things in motion more clearly than he could see objects at rest. His ancestors had been animals of prey, hunters, whose survival depended upon detecting the least movement in a still landscape, the flick of a hidden rabbit's ear, the stealthy creeping of a fox in a thicket.

But now Blaze discerned nothing except the closed door of an empty crate opposite him. In the confinement of the cage his eyes told him almost nothing, yet he did not feel the cage was a prison. Yesterday morning the invariable routine of his life had been suddenly disrupted; he had been taken away from everything he had known, and in this new and unexpected strangeness the cage had a certain familiarity, seeming to offer security, protection— his own lair. So much of his life, all the hours of the nights, had been spent locked in a cramped doghouse made of redwood boards with a solid door and only air holes for ventilation. The cage felt a little like home, in so far as he knew what a home might be.

His conscious memories spanned eight months of his ten-month life, and all of this time had been lived in a suburb of San Francisco, a flat anthill of a town teeming with ceaseless traffic that crisscrossed and circled, plunging into underpasses and tunnels, a seemingly mindless but eternal hurry. It was a town of small, individual houses on small, identical lots.

The suburb was a place without close destinations. There was no reason to walk to the corner or to the next block, for no shops, churches, or schools broke the unyielding monotony of the residential streets. There were neither paths nor sidewalks since no person was expected to go about on foot and no dog was allowed to. The shallow front yards of the houses ended at cement curbs bordering the blacktop.

At one side of every house stood a carport, roofed but unwalled except by the kitchen wall of the house. The dwellings were separated from each other by privet hedges, grape-stake fences, and the indifference or suspicions of the inhabitants.

Blaze had spent his entire daylight life pacing on a chain attached to a ring that slid along a heavy wire cable. The taut cable stretched between a corner of a house and an electric pole at the edge of its front yard, so the sliding ring permitted him freedom of movement to "defend" the streetside approach to the house; his dominion, the only ground his paws ever touched, was this territory running diagonally to the street, exactly twenty-two yards long and six yards wide.

By running wildly the length of the cable and back

again, as he did several hundred times each day, he covered the equivalent of several miles. His shoulders grew powerful and the hip muscles that propelled him on his endless beat back and forth hardened into steel springs.

The uniformly parceled, well-organized town with its civilized hydrangea beds and neat lawns appeared culturally advanced. It hardly seemed a place where public torture would be allowed; yet torture by intention and by neglect was almost a daily feature of Blaze's life, and his torments, taking place in view of a public street, went unnoticed.

The people of the town (they were too unconnected to be called "townspeople") paid little attention to what happened in their neighbors' yards. Indeed, the residents did not feel that they had neighbors, only that other people—strangers whose troubles were unknown—had addresses similar to their own. And even if Blaze's sufferings had been a matter of interest, there were no likely witnesses. Early every morning the men and women departed the town in a body to earn their livings, while great orange buses transported most children to faraway schools. The few infirm or encumbered, the baby sitters who remained behind, observed the world not through their windows but through the periscopes of their television aerials. So no one noticed, or at least no one protested, the torture of a German Shepherd Dog called Blaze.

Besides physical sufferings, the dog's strong natural affection went unreturned and ignored, a confusion of emotions welled in him, and he became indifferent before he turned angry. He did not feel that he belonged to anyone or lived with anyone, but rather that the house behind his territory was coincidentally occupied by two humans, the Jasmine Woman, who smelled like a harsh imitation of a plant that grew across the street, and the Onion Man who smelled like the vegetable growing wild behind the carport. The Onion Man or sometimes the Jasmine Woman provided him with food, and there was enough of it except on days when the house reeked of alcohol. At such times they forgot he was there.

He was unaware that they had names, that they were Mr. and Mrs. Blount, George and Wilma. Blaze did not have the least idea what a name was or that he himself had one, since the Blounts never spoke to him and seldom spoke to each other, finding it easier to communicate a few essential needs by nods, grunts, and unfinished gestures. Speaking to each other taxed them, perhaps because both the Blounts were stout and short of breath. Besides, after twenty years of sullen marriage there was little to say.

George Blount, who had never before possessed a dog, acquired this costly German Shepherd puppy by accident and somewhat to his surprise.

He worked as the foreman of the shipping department at a food-processing plant in the city and one day he was having lunch in the company cafeteria with several fellow workers when a salesman named Arthur Wheeler joined their table. This was flattering to George because Wheeler, whom he knew but slightly, ranked as one of the more important younger men in the company, a chief vendor of its products throughout a vast territory. He was seldom seen in the cafeteria, but when he did drop in, his attitude was always jovial and comradely.

Over coffee, talk at the table was about the sudden increase of crime in formerly safe suburbs, and George, who was concerned about this, told of two daring daylight burglaries in his own neighborhood.

"Moving vans came," he said, paling at the thought. "Big vans, and they took every stick of furniture in the houses. Tore the carpets right off the floors!" George went on, telling about his worry that such a thing might happen to his own home, until Arthur Wheeler interrupted him.

"George, this is your lucky day. I have the answer to your problem—a perfect answer."

George looked questioning.

"A guard dog! My wife's little nephew has been living with us since his parents were killed in a car accident. Just yesterday the boy's grandfather sent a puppy, a first-rate German Shepherd from one of the country's top kennels. A dog worth a lot of money."

"You're selling it?" George sounded alarmed.

"Certainly not!" Arthur Wheeler looked hurt at being so misunderstood. "My nephew's grandfather is crazy about these dogs. He's spent his whole life with them— breeds them on a ranch in the Rockies, trains them, judges them in some kind of competitions. He's famous among people who like that sort of thing. Maybe you've heard of him—Cappy Holland?"

"No. Odd name for a man, Cappy."

"A nickname. He's Captain Elias Holland. Long ago he was in the army, I think he was a founder of the Canine Corps—you now, they train dogs for military duty. Everyone calls him Cappy—it even appears that way in print in dog magazines my brother-in-law used to read.

"Anyway, he sent David—that's my nephew—this puppy. But we can't keep it in our apartment, the lease says no dogs in the building. I can't send it back or sell it without offending the old man. He's coming to California next spring and the first thing he'll ask is to see the dog. So I'm hoping to find a good home for it in the suburbs, a place where my nephew can visit it once in a while. And you seem to need a guard dog ... well ..." Arthur Wheeler smiled winningly, shrugged his shoulders, and made a little gesture indicating their mutual problem was solved.

Something stirred in George's dormant imagination, the flickering of an unaccustomed light. He saw himself as possessor of an animal of great distinction, a costly canine bred to guard the treasures of the rich and famous. Also, he liked the thought of getting better acquainted with Arthur, who one day would doubtless be in a position to grant favors.

"I'll take the dog," he said, and suddenly found himself shaking hands with Arthur.

Three days later the puppy, Blaze, was shackled in George Blount's patch of grass, secured with a chain heavy enough to hold a leopard. Arthur Wheeler, beaming a smile as boyish as the floppy bow ties he wore, bade George good-bye, promising to bring his nephew to play with the dog at some indefinite date. But Arthur was not as guileless as he appeared; he and his wife, Nadine, had agreed the night before that such visits would be upsetting to the boy, who might become too attached to the puppy.

During the months of growing up Blaze lived a life

without variation. Every weekday morning George Blount would release Blaze from the doghouse and immediately attach his collar to the chain in the yard. Usually George remembered to fill Blaze's water dish, but when he did not, the afternoons brought misery, the parched torment of thirst.

Even when the water dish was filled, a hot day meant suffering. Blaze's dense, harsh outer coat and the softer undercoat protected his skin from sunburn, but the direct rays of the sun often seemed unbearable. Since there was no shade, he dug pits in the yard so he could lie closer to the cooler earth. He groveled in these, panting and perspiring through his lolling tongue and through the pads of his feet. Blaze was only three months old when George Blount came home to find the lawn ruined, and he beat the puppy with a leather strap. The strap tore Blaze's flanks, seared him, but he did not resist because George, the Onion Man, was the bringer of food. Yet when the sun burned again, Blaze was compelled to dig once more. Eventually George gave up, deciding the dog was stupid. The thought of shade never crossed his mind.

The torments of heat, thirst, and confinement were hard to bear, but no less brutalizing was Blaze's loneliness. The pain of loneliness was vague and formless, a hunger he could not appease, undefined pangs that drove him to rage.

And at times when he drowsed in the yard, his paws flicked, his shoulder muscles twitched, as a dream unfettered him and he ran free, wild and joyous, dashing from lawn to lawn as he had seen the squirrels do, pursuing a sunbeam, chasing a shadow. He could run forever, far to the west or nearer to the east to the great stretches of water he knew about from the winds that brought their tantalizing coolness.

The dream of freedom was his greatest pleasure, just as his greatest punishment was the torment inflicted by his enemies, the three children.

The children came often in the late afternoons, small humans who made alarming moves and gestures—they darted, jerked, and capered. Such nervous, unsteady behavior was suspicious to Blaze, yet the first time he saw them approaching the yard, he instinctively felt gentle, an inner voice assuring him that these smaller creatures were not to be harmed or frightened. He felt strangely protective toward them.

But Blaze soon learned painfully that they came only to make a game of hurting him. Staying safely out of reach, they hurled stones and sticks. One of them had a bow and target arrows hard-tipped with metal, blunt yet hurtful. Blaze snapped the fallen arrows with one crunch of his jaws.

The children came close, stepping onto the lawn just beyond the limit of his chain, and the oldest little boy, knowledgeable about matches, lighted rolled newspapers, waved these torches as close to Blaze as he dared, then hurled them flaming at the maddened animal, screaming with excitement and triumph.

The children returned often, and slowly Blaze's besieged mind narrowed and focused: they were the enemy. The burning sun, the pangs of thirst, the Onion Man with his painful strap, all of these seemed as impersonal as the rain pelting him in the shelterless yard. But the children were enemies bent on his destruction, creatures whose pleasure was to hurt him, and he learned to hate them. One day they would venture too close, one day . . .

The Onion Man and the Jasmine Woman usually returned home about sunset, and when they arrived in the carport, their hair and clothing were permeated with the same smells that drifted from the distant city when the wind blew from the north.

Now and then people came to call at the house in the evenings or on Saturdays or Sundays. (Blaze knew the difference in the days of the week by the difference in events that took place on each of them, and he knew that the routine of the week was a cycle.) The dog sensed the Onion Man's delight when callers could not step into the drive or cross the yard until the Onion Man had put his hand masterfully and showily on Blaze's collar; also, the Onion Man conveyed pleasure when these guests were unable to leave unless he escorted them across Blaze's dread preserves.

"A born killer!" the Onion Man bragged. "I can only handle him because I feed him. Otherwise, he'd rip me limb from limb."

Blaze could not comprehend the words, but he recognized the pride, the approval in the man's voice, and knew what he had done to terrify the callers was right.

Then, one spring evening, a woman who was different from the other visitors came to call. She wore jangling silver jewelry and a cloth coat that flared and billowed behind her, all of which struck Blaze as suspicious and threatening. He did not trust things that waved or dangled or made unusual noises.

The woman left her car on the street, as callers always did, and reached the foot of the driveway as the Onion Man stepped from the house into the carport and called, "Just a minute, Marian, till I see to the dog."

"Oh, who's afraid of a dog," she retorted, coming forward with her chin high. "Shut up, mutt!"

Blaze, snarling and with fangs bared, lunged at the intruder, hurling himself with all his strength. Crying out in panic, the woman leaped backward, stumbled, and fell on the cement driveway. She lay out of his reach, but he caught her coat in his jaws and would have dragged her to him had not the cloth ripped, tearing a long strip from the coat, but freeing her.

"Vicious!" she cried, then made small wailing sounds. "Oh, oh, oh!" When she started to rise, attempting to wipe dirt and motor oil from her face, she wailed, "My ankle! Oh, my ankle! I've sprained or broken it."

Blaze, responding to her cries, lunged again, barking furiously.

"Quiet! Quiet!" shouted the Onion Man, thoroughly frightened. "I'm so sorry, Marian. Let me help you. Come inside and wash, and I'll make you a drink. Oh, I'll punish the dog, I promise you. I'll beat him within an inch of his life. I'm so sorry!"

"You should be!"

"Please don't let this spoil our evening. Wilma has supper ready. Here, take my hand."

The woman scorned his assistance. "My new coat's ruined! Do you have any idea what this coat cost at Magnin's? And my ankle! Somebody's going to pay for this and pay plenty, I can tell you."

"Now, now, it's all right!" Turning, he screamed at Blaze, "Shut up! Shut up! Stop that barking!"

"You invited me here, you're responsible for what that vicious cur does, George Blount! I'm seeing my lawyer tomorrow." She hopped on one foot to her car, still making whimpering cries of distress. "And shock, too. I think I'm in shock. Oh, how you'll pay for this!"

After she had gone, the Onion Man went into a frenzy. He cursed and kicked Blaze, chasing him up and down the cable, waving his arms and shouting. Twice he lost his balance and tripped, falling to the ground, still yelling and gesticulating.

Blaze endured the punishment, thinking he was being beaten for allowing the woman to escape, and he knew that in the future he must leap more quickly, strike harder and with less warning.

Two days later the woman's attorney reached George Blount by telephone at work, demanding a huge sum of money, warning him of impending legal action, and threatening criminal prosecution of George for harboring a vicious animal. Frantic, George tried to reach Arthur Wheeler, but the salesman was on the road and George had to wait three days in fear, expecting policemen and bailiffs to swoop upon him.

On the fourth morning Arthur, resplendent in a checked suit, found George at work near the great bins of onions and other vegetables.

"Congratulate me, George boy!" said Arthur, beaming. "I'm going to became a father. After six years of waiting, Nadine and I had given up hope. But now a blessed event is expected. Isn't that the greatest news?"

George mumbled congratulations, then burst into his story, pouring out a tale of anguish and danger. "The dog's crazy, just naturally mean," he explained. "I'll have him put away tomorrow. I'll call a vet—or do the police handle such things?"

Arthur's usually sunny face had darkened. "Just a minute! I told you long ago that my nephew's grandather was coming to San Francisco. Well, he'll be here in two weeks to judge some kind of dog exhibition, and he's going to want to see the pup. After that, I don't care what you do. I'll call this woman and calm her down, but you keep that dog two more weeks, understand?"

George could not have felt more threatened if Arthur had pointed a gun at him. "Sure," George agreed weakly. "I wouldn't let you down."

Two Sundays later Blaze was in the front yard when a camper chugged into the street, halted at the house, and an old man with very bright blue eyes climbed from the cab. Blaze challenged him, racing back and forth on the wire, uttering dire threats, but the old man did not seem perturbed. He stood quietly at the curb, arms folded, and did not set foot on the lawn.

He studied Blaze closely, watching every move, every leap and thrust, and at last nodded his head and gave a long sigh. He dropped slowly to one knee and began to talk gently, easily, his voice almost a singsong. Not once did he make a gesture, and his hands remained quietly folded.

Caught by the soft sound and suddenly curious about the man's immobility, Blaze stoped barking and listened, puzzled because no one had ever spoken more than a few words to him before. Both the man and the camper behind him gave off an old aroma of dogs, and the man's boots carried newer scents of strange animals, animals Blaze had never seen, but his instincts told him they were grazing creatures, not hunters; they were tame, not wild, and were not enemies. Another strange thing, the old man conveyed no sign or scent of fear, even though Blaze growled savagely.

"You're beautiful no matter how crazy they say you are! Too beautiful to be put to sleep, if it can be helped. But what can I do with you?" The voice became even softer. "I can't sell or give away a fellow as dangerous as you are, and I'm too old to start with another dog. Too old and too tired—and too hurt. I feel finished, Blaze. I'm too tired to go ahead, I can't stand still, and there's no way to turn back. I'm old and you're young, but we're in the same boat—no future at all."

The man reached into his shirt pocket and drew out a little ball of meat. With a slow, smooth gesture that was not alarming he tossed it at Blaze's feet. Blaze sniffed, pleased by the tempting perfume of hamburger, but fascinated by the unfamiliar aroma of dried liver mixed with it. He swallowed the offering at one gulp, then studied the man again, tilting his head to one side, puzzled by a dim stirring of memory, something he had once known but now no longer recognized.

"Was that good, Blaze? It had medicine in it, something to make you feel very peaceful and just a little sleepy."

The screen door of the kitchen slammed as George Blount entered the carport and crossed the lawn, smiling.

"Captain Holland?"

The old man gave a curt nod, but did not speak.

"I read that piece about you in the *Chronicle* yesterday." George was at pains to be affable. "Nice picture of you, too. Seems you've done everything there is to do with dogs."

"No, sir. Not everything. I have never brutalized one." Cappy Holland stared at the chain and cable with a baleful eye.

George blinked at him. It was hot, he suddenly realized, standing here in the sun, and he decided to cut the interview short.

"Well, Captain, this is the dog. I trained him to be a guard. Guess I trained him too well. I put out a fortune to feed him, then he turns vicious and attacks a woman."

Blaze, meanwhile, had stopped growling. Gradually he felt a sense of calm and well-being pervading his body. He was not really sleepy, although his vision seemed blurred, but enjoyed a novel sensation, a little dizzying yet not unpleasant.

When the old man came to him, he felt no anger, no stirring of defense or hostility. He stood serene while the studded leather strap that served as an imitation of a spiked collar was removed from his neck and replaced with a light slip chain. Blaze was not even upset when the old man took the heavy collar and, leaning back, hurled it furiously into the carport where it clanged against the garbage cans.

He saw the Onion Man retreating hastily, almost running, toward the house, and then Blaze went docilely to the van and entered the open cage with no protest.

Half an hour later they were in the city, and all the smells Blaze had known at a great distance, all the sounds that had been faraway echoes, now surrounded him, yet the world was pleasantly softened, muted by the peace and contentment he felt.

He slept then, and when he awoke in midafternoon he still felt quietly secure, but the sharpness of his senses was returning. Since he could not see outside the camper, it was a while before he understood that they were in motion. He knew this because of the sudden retreat of smells and sounds, a changing feast of odors such as he had never known before. The sharp freshness of eucalyptus rushed toward the camper, then withdrew, mingling with the passing aromas of newly cut grass and of animals who were guarded by another dog—grazing animals lingering near a cool pond whose moisture he felt high in his nostrils.

But he understood their progress not only by smell and sound; another sense, one he had not known he possessed, spoke to him for the first time. This sense told him of directions and distances, and the course of the journey became recorded upon his unconscious memory.

Meanwhile, he would hear the old man talking and sometimes singing in the cab of the camper, meaningless words, although one was repeated over and over: "Blaze

... Blaze ... Blaze ..." A soothing sound, yet a sense of unease, a suspicion, came to him, and finally he realized that he was not alone with the old man, that another human was present in the camper, one who made not the least sound or movement and was revealed only by the telltale scent he could not suppress.

A little later he saw this hidden passenger. They stopped at a place that smelled powerfully of gasoline and of oil drippings. Outside there was a confusion of motors starting and stopping, metallic clanks, and the *ping* of a small bell. The old man left the cab, slamming the door behind him, and in a moment there was a soft rustling in the far end of the van, followed by cautious footfalls.

Then Blaze saw him through the grating. It was a young boy, and he revealed the scent of fear as he reached for the big plastic water jug on the floor near Blaze's cage.

Blaze drew back, crouched with his back paws firmly under him, then hurled himself forward, snarling. His head and chest crashed against the door of the cage, which shuddered at his weight but did not yield. The boy fled back into hiding as Blaze tore at the grating with his nails and teeth, all the while in his mind attacking another boy, one who hurled painful stones and waved a flaming newspaper.

Finally, when they were again on the highway, the sound of the old man's voice in the cab lulled him, and as it grew dark, he slept. But it was a fitful sleep, for he knew he must remain alert, watchful. Soon the boy would attack the cage, would come to hurt him. Blaze was ready.

An hour went by and then another, night fell and still

they continued southward, down the long central valley of California. Very late they halted at a place near a river, a place with willow trees and a blossoming orchard. The old man left the cab to sleep a few hours in a tourist lodging, but returned a little before dawn. In the night the boy had again taken water from the jug, but this time, instead of challenging him, the dog lay quiet, pretending sleep, ready to hurl himself forward with rending fangs if, somehow, the door of the cage opened.

That morning they drove south again, south into the pale yellow dawn as they curved eastward. At length the old man halted the truck on the roadside, gave Blaze another pellet of meat, and when the feeling of peace and calm overcame Blaze's anger, he opened the cage and put in food and water, taking a few minutes to clean the floor with a liquid that smelled like cedar wood.

In the afternoon they left the main highway and took a road into the mountains. "It's out of the way a little, and it's winding," Cappy Holland told Blaze, speaking cheerfully from the cab. "But near the end of this road we'll see the nicest and prettiest lady in California."

Later he said, "Look, there's a hitchhiker, Blaze. We'd better stop for him. Another hour in this sun and he'll dehydrate, maybe turn into pure borax. We can't let that happen, can we, boy?"

And now, with the hitchhiker, they moved deeper into the desert. The feeling of sleepy tranquility was leaving Blaze, yet with each hour the cage and the camper became friendlier, more his own dominion, his to guard and defend. He lay quiet but alert, absorbing the journey, his senses bringing him messages the humans in the vehicle could not receive.

The sky was hidden from Blaze, so even if there had been dark clouds overhead—which there were not—he could not have seen them. Yet he knew that an electrical storm lay beyond the horizon, and that it moved toward them, riding the high winds above the southern mountains. An hour would pass before the others in the truck could suspect this, but Blaze felt the storm's lowered pressure on his eardrums like the falling of a barometer, and if he could not hear the rumble of thunder, he felt its vibrations as it echoed faraway, rolling over the canyons of stone below and through darker canyons of clouds in the churning sky.

Every breath of air told him of invisible animals concealed in the desert; for Blaze, this barren wasteland teemed with life. As the camper passed a hidden spring, Blaze knew that mule deer and desert sheep came here at night to water. The breeze brought news of wild horses grazing on the thin forage of an arroyo, and a cougar lurked in a deep culvert beneath the road.

Blaze lifted his head to the telling, flowing stream of air, and in a waking dream he was free now as once sleep had freed him from his chain. He bounded up the gravel-strewn slopes, his hard paws reaching out with great, long strides as though to dig the scattering sand, and his body was light, so weightless he might have sailed on the currents of air like the hawks that spiraled and drifted in the limitless, chainless sky.

He bounded in headlong, glorious pursuit, stampeding

the coyotes that peered unseen between the rocks on heights above the road; he raced the mule deer, put to flight the yellow quail; then, panting, rolling on his back, he twisted his tingling body, pawing the air like a puppy for the joy of being alive.

All the while, no matter how the road wound or curved, that steady, knowing compass in Blaze's brain recorded their track. With the need and freedom, he could have retraced his way up the long valley mile after mile, from town to town, through the confusion of the city to the suburb and have trotted into the yard of an astonished George Blount.

But he was already beginning to forget the Onion Man, although he would never forget the yard or any other place he had once known. His memory was keyed to his needs, to his survival, retaining all he required, discarding or diminishing the rest.

And he would never forget the children who had hurt him.

The scent of the boy hiding in the van came to him again, and he crouched in the darkness, watching and waiting.

Two

The road swung northeast, winding along the southern slopes of the saw-toothed Providence Mountains, skirting the edge of a valley so harsh and desolate that it had been proclaimed an Indian reservation for want of any other possible use.

The Green Hornet plunged into sudden dips, jolted, shook, and shuddered on the pavement that had buckled and broken where the road crossed long washouts or dropped into shallow arroyos where flash floods had gouged the land.

In the rear of the van, concealed by a doorless cupboard behind a hanging Navajo blanket, the boy David tried to stay at least half asleep and also tried to dream of snow.

He had seen snow, real snow, only once, two years ago when his father, realizing David had reached his eighth birthday without knowing true winter, took him and his mother to the high sierra in March. They spent three days at a ski lodge. His mother usually remained inside near a log fire, but he and his father almost lived on the slopes, sledding, making a giant snowman, and exploring white stands of pine trees. Only three days—but ever afterward it seemed to David that he and his father had spent weeks in the dazzling whiteness.

His life had changed completely at the end of that weekend. While they were returning to San Francisco, their car collided with a truck that had veered across the highway out of control. David's mother was killed instantly; David himself spent a year in various hospitals, learned to walk again, and was sent home the same month his father, Ben Holland, died from side effects of the accident.

So nothing was the same after the days in the snow, but David had only to close his eyes and that white world came back to him, shimmering and magical, dark branches of spruce trees bowed with winter weight, the flash of skate blades on the frozen lake in the valley, and great curling flakes drifting lazily like petals in the air.

Today was his second day of hiding in the van, and most of that time had been spent in the cupboard. Last night, while the van was parked among the willows, he had taken a long walk through open fields and orchards. The dog had raised a furious barking when he left and again when he returned, but the people in the tourist court where his grandfather slept paid no attention.

Now he huddled on the floor, curled almost into a ball, and although his thin cotton jeans were damp with perspiration and his pale forehead felt moist under the shock of dark hair, the heat of the cupboard did not bother him. He endured the heat, the cramped position, and the boredom of doing nothing with a silent patience that was completely unchildlike.

In the last two years, ever since that time in the snow and the accident afterward, he had learned how to be patient, how to lie still, how to close his eyes and let minutes melt to hours, fade to days, to weeks. He had learned those lessons held fast in traction, in hospital beds, and then in a wheelchair. He had been strapped and braced and pinioned. For what seemed to him a very long time he had been free of these restraints; he had even learned to run, although not very fast yet. But the lessons remained. He knew how to hold still.

The van dipped into another arroyo, bumping and rattling, and David's head bounced on the thin pillow he had made by folding the checked jacket his Aunt Nadine had insisted he wear when early yesterday morning she laid out his clothes for the bus trip to Redwood Ranch Boys' Camp. There was a big safety pin in the lapel of the jacket with which his aunt had attached a white card bearing a message:

Dear Mr. Bus Driver,
    This is David's first trip alone. Please be sure he gets off at Ukiah where people will meet him. Have a nice day!
Nadine Wheeler

A stupid note! It made him appear babyish, seeming to say he could not read signs in the stations himself, although he was over ten years old. He burned with mortification as he imagined a bus driver stooping down, seizing his lapel, and reading it. The man would then laugh, a laugh too loud and too full of false heartiness. He would probably pat him on the head and call him a "little man," which David hated.

But he did not argue with Aunt Nadine, knowing he would tear up the note the moment he was out of her sight. At the time she pinned the note to him it was still possible that he would really go to Redwood Ranch Boys' Camp.

That morning, yesterday, had been a terrible and dangerous time. For nearly three hours David had pretended he was willing, if not happy, to go to the camp, while at the same time his aunt was trying to hide her joy at her own plans to leave the city the moment David was gone. To complicate matters his grandfather was expected to pay a brief visit. "Today of all days!" Aunt Nadine said bitterly.

His clothes, newly tagged with name tapes, and the other things he would need for three weeks were packed in a blue and white striped duffel bag.

"A bag just like sailors always carry!" exclaimed his aunt gleefully, covering her nervousness with enthusiasm.

David knew better. Recently he had paid secret visits to the San Francisco embarcadero to scout possibilities of stowing away on a ship. He had seen many sailors, and they carried a variety of things—six packs of beer, bottle-shaped paper packages, and sometimes cardboard suitcases. But he had observed no striped duffel bags. In fact, they carried none of the things he longed to see, no brassbound sea chests or spyglasses, no parrots on their shoulders shrieking "Pieces of eight!" And he found no way to get past the chain-link fence and slip aboard a ship where he could hide himself in a lifeboat as he had seen a boy do on television.

"There, David!" she said gaily. "Your bag is ready, a big delicious lunch is packed. The bus ticket is pinned in your pocket, and the note on your jacket. You have your taxi fare and spending money. So you're all set to go!"

He gazed at her silently, unable to speak because he knew how happy she was that her own suitcase was packed and waiting in the bedroom, ready for her to leave to join Uncle Arthur at Lake Tahoe. "A second honeymoon!" she had said, describing it to a friend on the phone. "Just Arthur and I alone! Just the two of us." David had been listening on the extension; he knew all about it.

He had also been listening when she and Uncle Arthur had decided not to tell him about this special vacation they were taking. They had said they did not want him to feel left out, but Aunt Nadine added, "I just can't face another scene with him right now."

The scenes she spoke of were usually moments of silent savagery, and they came after he had heard her talking rapturously about "the new baby" or "our baby that's coming in the fall." He had never been what they wanted, he had been a substitute, and now he was an unneeded one.

When such thoughts came to him, he felt choked. But sometimes in his mind he saw the swirling snow, saw his father striding through the white flurries in a red mackinaw, wearing a wool cap with long dangling flaps called "hound's ears," which made David laugh because it was a funny name and the cap was funny looking. Closing his eyes, David seemed to feel himself lifted up, powerfully lifted, and he rode on his father's back down the shoveled path toward the doors of the ski lodge, where a great fire roared in the chimney.

His father had been dead for a year, and for so many months before his death he had seemed like a stranger, an unfamiliar man lying in a hospital bed. But Aunt Nadine's recent talk of the new baby somehow brought his father to life, as though at any moment a key would turn in the lock and his father would call out as he did so many evenings, "Where's that David? Where's David the Desperado?"

Perhaps the illusion came easily because he still lived in the same building, although in an apartment two floors below the one he and his parents had occupied. The size, shape, and plan of the apartments were identical; his bed and dresser were the same as always, and there was nothing strange in Aunt Nadine's taking care of him. She had always done so, his mother had not been strong, and since Uncle Arthur was absent on the road so much of the time, Aunt Nadine seemed always with them. In some ways she and his mother blended together in his thoughts, and he no longer knew which one had said what or given him which present or helped him mount a pony on the merry-go-round.

So he did not often miss his mother, and even memories of his father had lain quiet until three weeks ago when Aunt Nadine and Uncle Arthur had explained to him—happily, happily—that they were going to have a baby, a "little brother" for him.

Soon after this announcement David learned about the plan to banish him almost the moment his school term was over.

"Four wonderful weeks, David!" His aunt almost sang the words. "Then Uncle Arthur and I will come to get you."

He wondered if they really would, or if he even wanted them to. He would sit for hours at a window watching the ships move up the Bay toward the Golden Gate, ships bound for Japan, for Hong Kong and Singapore. But there was no way for him to go on one of the ships, nor would a log raft carry him down the Mississippi. It was a long time since he had believed in being swept away in a balloon to a magic planet, but during the hours alone in the apartment he thought of such things.

Dreams about his father came to him, dreams about things that he had once known but that were now vague and strange. He saw his father, who looked no taller than David himself, walking through a forest of giant sunflowers. This dream seemed important, but he did not know why.

Then, the night before he was to leave for the camp, he had overheard the plan for their private vacation when Uncle Arthur had called from Denver and David listened.

"You know, Nadine, we haven't been away together since David came to live with us," his uncle had said, and it seemed to David that there was a resentful note in his voice, a sound that had not been there before the announcement of the baby's coming.

In the morning at breakfast his aunt kept looking at her

watch, anxious, he supposed, for time to pass quickly, for him to leave. But it was his grandfather she talked about.

"The most inconsiderate man in the world!" She was not really speaking to David, but uttering her thoughts aloud as she often did. "He's been in town almost a week, so he certainly didn't have to wait until the last second to come here. I told him you had to catch an early bus, and that I have a million things to do. It isn't that he really couldn't make it earlier. He just doesn't care! Oh, the trouble Alice had with that man!"

Alice was his mother and Aunt Nadine never concealed the lack of affection between Alice and Cappy Holland. David knew very little about his grandfather, but in his mind the old man was a figure connected with disaster and tragedy. As far as he remembered, he had seen his grandfather three times. Long ago, when he had been too little to understand, he had been with his parents and his grandfather in a park, and hundreds, perhaps thousands, of barking dogs were in an open field.

"Don't touch them, David," his mother whispered fiercely. "Stay close to me, do you hear?"

The dogs were indeed frightening, especially when he saw that his mother was afraid. He had never realized before that any grown-up, especially a mother or a father, could be frightened. He screamed when some huge animal approached him, and for unknown reasons this caused a quarrel between his grandfather and his parents. His grandfather, he realized much later, had been ashamed of him for being a coward.

Then, long afterward when he and his father were in

different rooms in the same hospital, his grandfather had come to see them, but David remembered nothing about the visit except three red balloons tied to the foot of his bed.

The last visit was a year ago, at the time of his father's funeral, and because everything was confusing then, David's impressions were again vague.

The old man had looked down at him from a great height and said, "You look better than the last time I saw you. No more braces and crutches?"

"No," said David. "And I run better every day."

"Say 'No, Grandpa,'" Aunt Nadine interrupted.

"Grandpa?" The old man seemed quite annoyed; he glared fiercely and his cheeks turned red.

Later that day his grandfather thrust a small package into David's hands. He started to speak, then shook his head, and turning on his heel, stalked away.

The package contained a strange present, a ball not quite as large as a tennis ball and made of very hard rubber. If you dropped it, the ball made a faint *ding,* a ringing sound like a muffled chime. Presents, David supposed, were always new, and this ball was very old, pitted and scarred, with only traces of a green coating remaining.

Aunt Nadine looked at it with distaste. "Tooth marks!" she exclaimed. "Heaven only knows how many dogs have chewed on this thing—and what germs they had."

She carried it to the kitchen, holding it gingerly with her thumb and middle finger. David never saw the ball again.

He thought, although he was not quite sure, that it was

on that same day Uncle Arthur and Aunt Nadine had told him that he was to live with them always now; he was to be their own son—which was wonderful for them, they explained, because they had always wanted a son and now they had the perfect one, ready made.

David hardly thought about his grandfather until the end of the summer when Aunt Nadine, at lunch, made a grim announcement. "Your grandfather has sent us a dog."

"A dog?" A flicker of excitement such as he had not known in a long time made David's eyes widen. "Where is it?"

"Still at the airport, but they're sending it here. Thank goodness your uncle will be back tomorrow."

"Can we keep it?" David held his breath.

"Oh, David, you know very well we can't," she said gently. "You're not strong enough to take care of a dog."

"But I am! And if it's just a puppy—"

She shook her head. "We can't have dogs in this building, it's in the lease. Believe me, David, I'm sorry."

David saw the puppy only once and very briefly because Mr. Kucharski, the janitor, did not like to be bothered. The dog had been delivered and was being kept in the basement of the building in a crate made of fiberglass with a barred door; its lonely howling filled David with strange and disturbing emotions as he approached cautiously. The basement was dim and the cage so dark that David could see little, but when he put his fingers between the bars, the puppy stopped his howls. A small, red tongue kissed David's fingers, and for several minutes the boy sat quietly, not moving his hand, pervaded by a warmth that made him smile.

Mr. Kucharski returned. "I have to lock up now," he said. "And tell your folks I didn't get a wink of sleep last night, what with all that howling."

Two days later, when Uncle Arthur told him that the dog had "a wonderful home in the suburbs," tears suddenly dimmed David's eyes. Uncle Arthur realized he was about to cry, and it startled him, because somehow David always managed to hold back tears.

"Now you mustn't be selfish," Arthur Wheeler said firmly. "The puppy will have a big yard to play in! He can be outdoors all the time on soft grass. How can you be sad when you know what a happy life he'll have and how cooped up he'd be here?"

The puppy was never mentioned again, but now David sometimes thought about his grandfather and about the mountain ranch where the puppy had come from. "He raises them," Aunt Nadine told him. "He lives surrounded by dogs. Dogs on the couch, dogs in his bedroom, even dogs in the kitchen, I suppose. Why Alice used to say she wouldn't be surprised if fifteen dogs sat down at the table with him."

It was a peculiar but a very funny idea. David imagined a long banquet table with a white cloth. Dogs sat sternly in highbacked chairs, linen napkins tucked under their collars. His grandfather presided, and although there was perfect order at the table, the old man had a whip and a chair like those Fearless Lothar used when he tamed lions in the Shrine Circus.

He thought of his grandfather as Christmas approached, deciding that the present he was sure to receive would signal his grandfather's feelings, perhaps show that he was less indifferent to David than he had seemed and than Aunt Nadine somehow indicated. In books and stories elderly men were very fond of their grandchildren. Grandfathers were supposed to enjoy telling stories about how it was when there were Indians. They taught you how to draw maple syrup from tree trunks and other useful things, although somehow David could not quite picture his own grandfather in this role.

But the answer seemed apparent when Christmas came and went and no present at all arrived. "Not even a card!" his aunt remarked to his uncle, when she thought David was out of hearing. "And to think we sent him that nice necktie and a box of handkerchiefs in David's name."

Then, surprisingly, two days after his tenth birthday in March, a package from his grandfather arrived. It contained a long narrow whistle made of shining steel and attached to a sturdy chain.

"How thoughtful of Cappy," said Aunt Nadine, a grim note in her voice. "Just like three years ago when he sent the drum and the harmonica."

But the whistle proved defective. No matter how hard David blew, it made only the faintest sound.

"Now isn't that too bad!" exclaimed Aunt Nadine, and she bought him fancy dominoes to make up for the disappointment.

David put the whistle away in the cigar box with his broken compass, the battery-powered model race car that would not run, the keyless padlock, and other valuables. But he sensed some mystery about the whistle, a feeling that his grandfather had sent more than just a broken toy.

He forgot about the whistle then, forgot the dogs, and did not think of his grandfather until one day Aunt Nadine said, "Your grandfather's coming to San Francisco, but I don't know how you'll have much time with him. You have rehearsals for the school pageant, then the performance on Friday and the end-of-semester picnic on Saturday. Then on Sunday morning you leave for camp."

"Yes, camp," he said. "Maybe I should go later on."

She did not hear him, she was looking thoughtfully at pictures of maternity dresses in a magazine. "Well, it's not our fault Cappy's coming at such a bad time."

But his grandfather's arrival was practically forgotten in the days that followed, and even on the Sunday morning when he was expected at any moment, other matters loomed in David's mind. Was Redwood Ranch Camp really just a camp or was it an orphanage, a home for unneeded children who had been replaced?

Suddenly Aunt Nadine was kneeling beside him. "Oh, David, you won't be lonely at camp, will you? Your Uncle Arthur and I want you to have a wonderful time. You do know we love you, don't you?"

He saw tears in her eyes, and this terrified him, for if she cried, he would begin crying, and then everything would come out about listening on the extension, and Uncle Arthur's wanting to go away without him, and how he realized no one wanted him and there was no place to go.

But the angry sound of the buzzer from the lobby saved

him. Aunt Nadine rose quickly, patting her hair, dabbing at her eyes with a tissue. "That's Cappy now. Remember, David, you're to say, 'I'm happy to see you, Grandpa.' And kiss him on the cheek. I know how you hate to kiss people, but be nice just this once. Please, David."

He would not do it. She couldn't make him. And his grandfather, who didn't like him, could go to the devil!

But then his grandfather strode into the apartment as if he were striding down a mountain, and David stared at him, too startled and fascinated to be angry.

The entrance hall seemed too narrow and too low-ceilinged to contain him. When he said, "Hello, Nadine, how are you?" his voice brought the outdoors inside, and the room, big a moment ago, was suddenly cramped. David half remembered stories his father had told him, stories about canyons where you found piñon nuts and about horses galloping through shallow streams, their hooves flinging the water into the sunshine so that for an instant tiny rainbows danced in the air.

"Cappy, how good to see you!" Aunt Nadine shook the extended hand.

"Hello, David. I gather you've been a busy fellow this week. Too bad. We had a fine obedience trial yesterday. I hoped you'd see it, but your aunt said you'd be heartbroken to miss the school picnic."

David looked up at the weathered face as they shook hands. Because he could think of nothing else to say, he said, "Thank you for the whistle, even if it doesn't work."

"Doesn't work?" His grandfather frowned. "How would you know? That's a whistle only dogs can hear.

Don't tell me you've got ears like a dog? Your aunt and uncle would never get over it!"

David began to smile, then realized that this was somehow not quite a joke.

"When I sent the whistle, I thought you still had a dog. I have since learned by telephone that I was mistaken."

Looking at his grandfather's cold eyes, David suddenly felt guilty of an unknown but enormous offense. "Would you like to have the whistle back?"

"No, I have others." Leaning down, he read the note pinned to David's lapel. "Well, well! That should melt anybody's heart."

"Would you like some coffee?" said his aunt, her voice tense. "I'm sorry Arthur isn't here. I told you he's in Denver, didn't I?"

Over coffee his aunt and his grandfather talked of people and times David did not know. It was an uneasy conversation, punctuated by awkward silences. As he listened to the old man's gruff voice, to the terse questions and brief replies, he felt more and more certain that he did not like his grandfather.

He was afraid of him—afraid and in awe. Yet he felt a yearning for the old man's approval, or if not approval, at least acceptance. But his grandfather seemed deliberately to avoid glancing in David's direction, and David tried to think of something to say that would draw attention to himself, something clever that would make the old man smile or even nod admiringly. But nothing came to his confused mind, and he sat staring dumbly at his own shoelaces. But as he listened, no longer paying attention to the words, he recognized a quality in Cappy's voice, a certain tone, that was hauntingly familiar. He thought of his father; he thought again of the snow.

Aunt Nadine looked at her watch. "Oh, dear, I'm afraid David has to hurry down to the taxi stand now or he'll miss his bus."

They all stood up. There was a silence, and David knew the moment of expulsion had come. He resisted a sudden, wild impulse to throw himself on the floor, to kick the carpet with his heels while he shouted rage and defiance. He would not go, would not go!

"I'll be on my way in a moment, too, Nadine. There's a long trip ahead of me. But first, I'll need the address of this fellow who has my dog."

"Your dog?"

"Of course. The papers are still in my name. Actually, I'm co-owner with David. I never sign away a fine dog until I feel sure. This time I'm sure—but in the opposite way."

"Of course." She was flustered. "And I'll give you a map of how to get there, just as soon as David's on his way."

David solemnly shook hands with his grandfather. "Come back soon," he said, and the words came out as a whisper.

"No, I'll not be here again," said the old man. "Maybe someday you'll come to Spirit Canyon."

It was not an invitation, and instead of a smile, Cappy's face held a look of sadness and farewell as he gazed down at David. *He* knows, David thought. He knows I hate going to this camp; and he knows why I'm being sent there. He knows everything. That's why he's sorry and why he pities me. And being pitied, although he pitied himself, seemed more than he could bear.

Aunt Nadine was bombarding him with last-second worries and cautions; she fluttered around him, waving her hands, brushing his cheek with a kiss, but he was hardly aware of her, and he forgot to say good-bye. Carrying his lunch box and the duffel bag, he went down to the lobby and then to the street. Nothing was clear to him, he did not know where he was going, what he would do.

The click of the latch behind him was like a signal. When he came back to this door, if he ever came back, the world would be different, utterly changed. He tore the note from his lapel, ripped it into tiny pieces, and let the breeze carry them away. But the destruction did not give him its promised pleasure; it even seemed unimportant. Was Aunt Nadine already on the telephone telling Uncle Arthur that they were rid of him?

David moved a few steps toward the taxi stand, then halted suddenly, his attention caught by the ancient truck with the out-of-state license plates. The daisies and sunflowers painted on the sides were faded but gay, and they smiled at David, who could not smile back. Could a man as cross as his grandfather have done this painting, even have imagined the great emerald green insect with long-lashed pink eyes that hid among the blossoms?

His father spoke in a distant memory, a memory like a dream. *"The sunflowers grow by the stone rim of the old well. When I was little, I thought I'd never grow as tall as the sunflowers."*

Without thinking, he turned the knob of the back door

of the van, and he was startled when the door opened invitingly at his touch. Then, still without conscious thought, he put his striped duffel bag and the lunch box on the floor inside, and knowing this was what he was meant to do, he mounted the two steep steps.

Near a giant saguaro cactus that resembled a statue of a many-armed Hindu god, Cappy Holland pulled the van onto a narrow shoulder, easing it cautiously as though testing for quicksand. Just ahead and to the right stood a big weather-beaten sign, its boards so warped and its paint so faded that it might have been the billboard counterpart of the Green Hornet: it had seen better days, but not for a long time.

Just 40 Miles To
Clean Beds At
MISS MYRNA'S STATE-LINE
CABINS
Last Chance to Avoid the Mann Act

"Nice lady, Miss Myrna," said Cappy. Reaching under the seat, he found a wide-mouthed vacuum bottle and, opening it, took out three small gray cubes of cooked meat. "Fried liver. It spoils fast, but no matter what they invent, it's still the best bait in the world."

"Bait?" The hitchhiker, who knew something about fishing, looked doubtful. The old man's mind was wandering again, he decided. Or did he mean bait for some kind of trap?

Cappy took a bottle of pills and a Swiss army knife from the dashboard. He broke a pill in half, expertly cut a slit in one of the liver cubes, and inserted half a pill.

"A tranquilizer," he said. "I want to take that boy back there out for a little run in about twenty minutes, and I don't want to take any foolish chances. He's plenty spooky."

The hitchhiker gave him an apprehensive look. So the little boy was being kept drugged. The whole thing was crazy, dangerous.

The old man left the cab, opened the rear door of the van and returned a moment later. "He went for it like a starved crocodile. In a little while I'll be safe handling him, but after another hour or two he'll probably revert to his savage self."

The hitchhiker nodded, hopelessly confused.

They approached another large road sign, and this one, like its predecessor, looked ancient and wind-worn, the lettering eroded and almost erased by the dust storms of years.

AT MISS MYRNA'S
Best Beer & Wine Since Omar K.
"Come Fill The Cup & In The Fire Of Spring
Your Winter Garment Of Repentance Fling."
Free Cups!   Free Matches!
Bring Your Own Garments

The old man pointed to the sign. "I'll be stopping there for the night. You can probably hitch a ride there, or if you don't mind a little hike, it's only half a mile or so to the main highway."

"Fine." Miss Myrna's, the hitchhiker thought, should just suit the old man. Judging from the signs, the place was as crazy as he was. Whatever Miss Myrna's turned out to be, he could not see it soon enough. He felt more and more convinced that the old man was up to something criminal, and the last thing he wanted was to be mixed up in his ultimate arrest. Or perhaps his seizure by white-coated men from the asylum.

"Damnation! Now look at that!" The truck shuddered to a halt. On the left a rock-strewn slope rose sharply to the wall of a cliff, and below the cliff, fifty yards from the truck, stretched a flaring spread of desert marigolds—yellows, ochers, browns, and every shade of gold, a bonfire of color in a landscape of grays and duns.

The old man sat quietly a moment, gazing out the window, then checked the watch that was fastened to his wrist with a heavy leather strap. "Time for the next round with Blaze—and I hope that pill is working," he said with a sigh, then spoke to the hitchhiker. "Be patient a few minutes, young man, then we'll be whizzing down the highway again. Right now my newest problem in life needs exercise."

"I'll just stretch my legs, too," said the hitchhiker, reaching for the door handle.

"Hold it right there, young fellow!"

The hitchhiker's head snapped toward the old man, and he almost expected to see a drawn six-shooter.

"If you have an urgent natural need to leave the cab, do

it now while he's still locked up and I'll wait for you. But once he's *out*, you stay *in!*"

The hitchhiker nodded quickly and denied he needed to leave the cab at all.

When the old man stepped down and carefully closed the door behind him, the hitchhiker realized he was taller than he had appeared, well over six feet. He vanished from sight, and the hitchhiker, getting on his knees, turned backward on the seat to peer through the mesh-covered window. The door of the van opened and sunlight flooded the interior.

The old man did not climb inside, but sat on the threshold near the first of the six boxlike cages and leaned toward the bars. He was greeted by snarls and growls, but they were not so savage as before.

He talked quietly to the caged animal, and his voice did not carry to the cab except for the repeated word "Blaze." It must be a dog he was cajoling, and the hitchhiker knew nothing whatever about dogs except that they terrified him. Only a month ago a nasty cocker, sensing his aversion, had retaliated by wetting on his new suede shoes.

Several minutes passed, and the old man, who seemed to have endless patience, continued talking softly. Then, when the snarling had ceased, he reached out very slowly and unlatched the door. The hitchhiker gasped, not knowing what mayhem to expect.

Then the animal's head and part of its body emerged, and the hitchhiker recognized the beast as what he called a "police dog," a dog that looked like Rin-Tin-Tin, whose adventures he had seen in an old movie on television, a film he had not liked. He felt deathly afraid of such dogs, vividly recalling stories about their devouring babies alive, turning on beloved masters, and slashing the throats of civil rights protesters.

But seeing this animal in the sunlight from the open door—and with a steel mesh safely between them—the hitchhiker realized that the dog was oddly beautiful, although his first impression was more of drama than beauty, perhaps because the strong, erect ears gave the animal such an alert appearance, a look of being poised for action. The thick coat gleamed, and the back, which at first glance appeared to be jet black, was actually shot with threads of fine silver; on the throat, below the long muzzle, a patch of white stood out like an Elizabethan collar. As the dog moved, slowly and suspiciously out of the cage, the hitchhiker saw that its legs and lower chest were coppery, almost a burnt orange, as dark as the darkest marigolds on the slope above.

Startled by the appearance, by the flash of silver and white, the gleam of dark gold, the hitchhiker momentarily forgot to be afraid, and watched in fascination as the old man slipped a light chain over the dog's head, all the while continuing a soft, soothing patter. "That's my boy, Blaze, we'll take a walk in the marigolds . . . but you don't know about walks, do you? Or about leads or slip chains. . . . Let's go now, Blaze. . . . Come with me . . . Oh, you don't know about steps, do you? Or about jumping down them. What a terrible education you've had! Poor fellow! . . . Come on, Blaze. . . . See what I've got here? That's liver. Doesn't it smell good? Come and get the liver, but just don't take my hand off with it. Oh, it's good liver, but my hand's old and tough and has no flavor at all—you wouldn't like it a bit. Come on, Blaze. . . . Ah, that's a boy!"

Then the two of them were walking side by side up the shallow slope toward the marigold patch. And suddenly, to the hitchhiker's surprise, the old man began to run, a curious loping run, knees bent, his strides very long and smooth, giving an impression of great speed although he was actually not covering much ground.

"Freaked out," muttered the hitchhiker.

The dog, despite being confused by the leather lead attached to the slip chain, moved briskly at his heels, then raced ahead. The old man dropped the lead and sat on the ground, panting and wiping his forehead while the dog bounded in great circles, joyfully barking. With a yelp of pure abandon, he hurled himself straight into the air, flipping over as he fell to the ground, landing on his back and kicking for sheer happiness. Then, upright once more, he raced and capered and cavorted, chasing a butterfly, plunging after a locust, giddy with the freedom of a vast, undiscovered world.

The hitchhiker, seeing an opportunity, spoke through the mesh to the back of the van. "Boy? Where are you, anyhow?" No answer came, no sound in the cages or from behind the Navajo blanket. "I know you're there! What's the matter with you? Why don't you answer?" Silence.

A few minutes later the old man returned, the dog following him and seeming content to go back to its cage.

When the old man entered the cab, he was carrying a

hatful of marigolds. "For a lady," he said, and started the motor, which caught after several strangled attempts.

"It's tricky trying to exercise a sedated dog," he remarked to no one in particular. "If you're wrong about the amount or the timing, the dog won't move. Well, I never approved of tranquilizing anyway, and that's the last pill I'll give him. About one more feeding, and I should have his confidence. If he isn't completely loco!" He shook his head and smiled into space, then turned to the hitchhiker and said in a voice almost fierce, "Did you see that dog move?"

"Yes," said the hitchhiker, wondering what he was supposed to say. Of course it had moved.

"Did you see those front paws *dig* as he reached out? What a gait! Smooth! He looks like he could run from here to Texas and never stop for breath!"

"It's a police dog, isn't it?"

"No," replied the old man sternly. "He's a German Shepherd Dog—and he's the best damn dog you're ever likely to see, young man." Then he relented a little. "Of course, they're used for police work. In a way it's a pity they're so good for police duty and as war dogs. People forget that practically all seeing-eye dogs are German Shepherds, and they're so gentle and wise and patient that they're the next thing to a new pair of eyes. Most search-and-rescue dogs are Shepherds, too. But people forget how sweet and helpful they are. And how beautiful." He paused a moment. "Ah, yes, how beautiful! I suppose that's why a person gets involved with them in the first place. Not because they're intelligent or useful, but because they fill your eye."

The hitchhiker thought of the six cages behind him. "Do you own a lot of those dogs?"

"No," said the old man gruffly. "Not any more."

Thunderheads were piling up in the southwestern sky when they arrived at the junction of two state roads. An hour remained before twilight, but the day had lost its brightness and turned cool quite suddenly. On the left, parched and treeless, huddled a cluster of small ramshackle buildings dominated by a huge sign.

AT LAST MISS MYRNA'S!
Cabins Restaurant Curios
Famous 1 Pump Gas Emporium
Jugs Iced Tires Checked Fortunes Told
The Hottest Chili This Side of Hell

A stake truck stood parked near the lone gas pump and a man, apparently the driver, prowled around the vehicle, squinting at the tires.

"I suggest you approach that gentleman for a ride," Cappy told the hitchhiker. "If he turns you down, I'll take you on to the interstate junction. That's the main highway and there's a fancy truck stop there. Lots of traffic."

"Thanks," said the hitchhiker, hurriedly picking up his backpack. "That'd be kind of you."

"Kind nothing! You think I'd let anybody get caught in the storm that's coming? Look at those clouds! Go on now, and good luck."

The hitchhiker darted from the cab, spoke briefly with the driver of the stake truck, then waved good-bye to

Cappy, who watched until the truck, bearing the hitch-hiker, pulled out and moved down the highway.

"An odd young man," he said aloud. "Peculiar!" He felt relieved to be rid of a passenger he had not quite trusted for the last two hours. "Appears to be seeing things," said Cappy, deciding the hitchhiker was a little crazy. "You meet strange people nowadays."

He parked the van where it would not block the gas pump or the entrance to the lunch-counter restaurant, then for a moment sat quietly leaning against the steering wheel, gazing at the desolate but dearly familiar place with a mixture of pleasure and suppressed dread at what he might find.

In the five years since he had last stopped here little seemed to have changed. The buildings, some clapboard, some cinder block, were slightly older, slightly shabbier, more run-down and out-of-date—just as I am, he thought.

Why expect great changes? After all, five years were so few compared to the more than forty that had passed since he first drove into the graveled entrance of Miss Myrna's. Everything had been new then, and the fresh green and white paint gleamed with false optimism, the never-to-be-kept promise of getting rich by fishing the stream of travelers flowing past the door. Miss Myrna's father had died the year before, and she had invested her small inheritance in this bright dream, only to see her hopes doomed when the new highway was built farther south, leaving the lunch counter, the gimcrack cabins, the shelves of Indian curios and picture postcards marooned and forlorn. Why, he wondered, had she stayed here? He had never believed her first answer, "Oh, I suppose the desert gets a hold on you."

Later on—twenty years ago? thirty?—he had pressed her about this. "Someday I'll go," she said. "Sometime."

A saying came to his mind. *"Through the street of by and by we arrive at the house of Never."*

Suddenly her anger blazed. "Then you've found your answer—never! They'll carry me away in a pine box. Where else would I go? Are you taking me with you? Is that what you're asking me?" And of course he was not. He never questioned her again.

He tried to remember parking in this spot the first time. No, not this spot. He had stayed farther away, conscious that he could not afford a cabin, that he would sleep in the cab of the truck. But he went to the restaurant hoping to pay to take a shower.

Would he now recognize that innocent young man who went inside twisting a dime in his pocket? Yes, he would know him, but doubted he would like him very much. It takes patience to put up with a starry-eyed boy, especially when that boy has already reached his mid-twenties and has learned nothing.

The truck he drove then was neither more nor less battered than the one he drove now—in the automotive department of life, he had exactly held his own. There had been four German Shepherds in the back, his slightly famous canine quartet of obedience champions, and they were all bound for Hollywood to become movie stars. Tucked away in the coat pocket of the decent blue suit that hung wrapped in newspapers was a letter from the great film producer who had, by accident, seen his dogs perform at an obedience trial.

". . . Your fantastic training . . . those noble animals of vast intelligence . . . will follow in the tracks of Strongheart and Rin-Tin-Tin. . . . When you come to the Coast, call me . . ."

And, oh, but that quartet was beautiful! Heidi, who could clear a fifteen-foot broad jump at a height of four feet, sailing like Pegasus; Inga, who took commands so fast she seemed to read his mind; and the two magnificent males, both dual champions for obedience and beauty, Donner and Blitzen. What a show they put on—tracking, leaping, retrieving, scaling a wall.

Yet they were never "trick dogs," never for an instant circus performers. Their young owner, blindly proud of them though he was, at least knew better than to degrade them by transforming them into grotesque parodies of humans—walking on two legs, dancing, catching baseballs while they wore funny caps.

There had been so many puppies since then, but those four, his first loves, remained unchallenged in his heart. He could still feel Donner's soft nose gently touching his arm to awaken him in the morning and, opening his eyes, he could see Donner's dark golden gaze studying him gently, thoughtfully, for Donner was the studious one, the quiet scholar of the quartet, just as Heidi was a loving clown, while Inga, who was fussy and precise, had no sense of humor whatever. Blitzen, a roughneck who disgraced them all with horseplay, made up for this by his adoration of Cappy.

His quartet—copper and silver and jet and steel and lightning and love.

So, after their first victories, they were going to be Hollywood stars. He had believed such things then. Worse, he had even believed they might be important.

The first time he entered the restaurant its dimness had blinded him after the glare of the sun outside. A bell hanging over the door tinkled and, as at a signal, a pack of small dogs raced from behind the counter, a herd of miniature poodles swirling about him, snapping at his boots, leaping straight into the air as if they had springs for paws, meanwhile still in full cry.

A woman's voice shouted, "Annette, Cecile! Yvonne! Marie! Shut up, all of you! Be quiet Emilie!" As Cappy heard the French names, so famous just then, he realized the puppies numbered five.

Then he looked at the woman behind the counter, looked into that strange, arresting face he would never forget, yet could never describe or define. At first glance her features were too severe, the eyebrows stern, the hair skinned back too primly in a tight bun. The word "schoolteacher" came to his mind, and he later learned he had been right. She was "Miss Myrna" who until last year had restlessly taught fourth grade in Riverside. But the nose and cheekbones that were too strong also gave her an exotic look, and his second thought was not of a schoolteacher but of a gypsy. She had knowingly emphasized this with small gold ear loops and a touch of gaudy eye shadow. He could not remember when he decided she was beautiful.

"I hope you like dogs, mister," she said. "Because dogs are something we have plenty of."

"I like dogs," he told her and bent to pet one of the poodles, which promptly bit him. (Years later it struck him as odd that of the hundreds of powerful dogs he had trained, of the thousands of strong muzzles he had examined as a judge, none had ever bitten him; the only dog that had—and it was a nasty bite—was a twelve-pound miniature poodle wearing lavender ribbons.)

She treated the wound with iodine, swabbing his hand. Then staring intently at the lines of his palm, she said, "I tell fortunes. Shall I tell what I see ahead for you?"

He smiled uneasily. "I'm afraid I couldn't pay you, miss."

"Miss Myrna," she corrected him. "I know you can't pay—it's in the lines of your palm." She was now holding his hand in both of hers. "Everything's there, and I have great power. I see how you will meet a dark stranger, a woman, a gypsy with golden earrings . . ."

So instead of sleeping in the truck, he slept in a cabin, and the next morning when he asked her to marry him, she could not quite hide her laughter until she saw how much it hurt and shamed him.

"I'm older than you," she said, pain and tenderness in her eyes.

"What's a year or two?"

"No, a hundred years. And I was born to be alone."

"You weren't alone last night."

She did not answer, but something in her expression denied their closeness, and as she turned away, he saw just the edge of a look so empty and lonely that he took her in his arms as though she were a weeping child and begged her, "Don't be alone, don't be alone." He did not know why, but he was deeply afraid for her, and young enough and foolish enough not to be afraid for himself.

Afterward he could not remember exactly what she said that consoled him, but three days later, when very gently she made him leave, he felt undiminished by her rejection.

Two years later he returned, defeated, hating himself because his dream of Hollywood had proved infantile and he had learned he could not cope with the fierce world, he was ignorant and defenseless. Blitzen, the loving roughneck, was dead, and when he looked at the three survivors of his wonderful quartet, he felt pain and desperation because they were almost as thin as he was.

She helped give him back his confidence, made him feel that he was a man again. That summer the swarthy mechanic who worked the gas pump held her interest, but she concealed this and Cappy learned about it years later when such things no longer mattered to him.

She represented the landmarks of his life, although he had seen her infrequently. Each visit had been special. She had admired him in his army uniform, dithering over his captain's bars, and listened to his unabashed bragging about the dogs he was training for war. Miss Myrna had known Ben, his son, but had never met his wife, although after his wife's death he had come here and felt less lonely for a while—then she made him know it was time to move on, that his life was elsewhere.

And now the last visit.

Taking the marigolds from his cap, he gathered them into a rough bouquet. He suddenly found he was tired, worn out from the long drive, and although he did not quite admit it, his bones ached from running with Blaze.

And he was hungry, even imagining he smelled the aroma of hot coffee from the restaurant. Climbing down from the cab, he felt a petty irritation that the dog's needs must come before his own. But all his life he had believed that no man should sit down at a table until his animals had been fed.

Not animals now. Only one, he thought, opening the door of the van. Only one—but one too many for him.

Thunder rolled across the sky and Blaze, intently watching Cappy through the barred door, pricked up his ears, but gave no other sign.

"So you're not spooked by the thunder, fellow? That's good," said Cappy. Deftly, without thinking about what he was doing, he mixed the food in a metal dish. "Maybe you're so quiet because of the pills, but that ought to be wearing off. Had a good nap, Blaze? Oh, I see you're hungry. Well, so am I."

Cappy unfastened the door of the cage, unworried about the dog, knowing that in these circumstances he was identified in Blaze's mind as the bringer of food. Later this might change—Cappy was too experienced to trust Blaze with a full stomach—but right now he did not worry about the dog's disposition to attack. Still, he put the pan on the floor before opening the door, not tempting Blaze to leap for it and perhaps catch a hand by mistake.

Cappy glanced around the interior of the van. "Well, I guess there's no reason for you to go back in that cage right away, and I won't wait till you finish eating. You can have the run of the van for a while."

David, crouched in the cupboard, heard the words but did not understand their meaning. He did not even realize that the dog was not in his cage when his grandfather left the van and closed and locked the door behind him.

Three

Cappy, seeing her through the screen door, stopped at the threshold, surprised. Like a gauze curtain, the wire mesh softened and slightly blurred his view of the room beyond. Miss Myrna, slender as a girl, stood behind the Formica lunch counter, frowning through thick glasses as she poured salt from a cardboard box into a shaker. Except for the heavy glasses, which he had not seen before, she appeared unchanged by the years, her black hair as thick and lustrous as ever, her forehead unlined. At her ears and wrists gold gypsy loops sparkled in the cold fluorescent light.

Pushing open the door he heard, as he had always heard, the tinkle of a bell, then the shrill barking of a pack of tiny dogs. They swept from behind the counter—six dogs? No, a swarm of seven charged toward him, yelping excitement and welcome. Their delicate paws and sparkling eyes were poodlelike, but over the years Miss Myrna's pack had evolved into a breed apart.

Still concentrating on filling the salt shaker, she gave a

nod of automatic greeting. "I hope you like dogs, mister. Because dogs are something we have plenty of."

As the words echoed across forty years, Cappy waited silently, hardly breathing, feeling for that moment young again, almost boyish as he stood holding his unruly bouquet of wild flowers.

"Cappy!" she cried then, and salt spilled across the counter. "Cappy! Oh, Cappy!"

They embraced while the swarm of black dogs swirled at their feet, yipping high-pitched approval, leaping straight into the air, bouncing like woolly balls. Artfully Miss Myrna slipped the thick glasses into her apron pocket.

She prepared his supper, a steak burned on one side and gray on the other for she forgot to turn it over, and a mound of potatoes with onions. After serving him in one of the two booths, she drew herself a mug of faintly brown coffee and sat opposite him, delighted at his praise of the food, touched by his gift of flowers. Talk came so easily to them that they might have seen each other only the day before.

"And you look wonderful," he told her. "Younger every year."

She shook her head. Times had not been good, she told him. For a while she had been in a hospital—"for too long."

"But you're all right now?"

"Yes. I'm all right now." Her tone was so final, so forbidding of any questions that he looked at her sharply, noticing now that her cheeks were gray beneath two wings of bright rouge. Yet the sparkle in her eyes, her laughter, her quick little gestures were so vivacious that Cappy thought uneasily of those mountain gentians whose blue is most brilliant just after the first touch of the frost that will destroy them.

"Tell me everything," she said, touching his hand across the table. "It's been almost three years since you were here, hasn't it? Oh, Lord, no! Not three, but five!"

Outside rain began to fall, big drops splashing against the plate glass windows. "Ben and Alice were in an accident," he said at last. "She was killed. He died over a year ago."

"I know. You wrote me a note."

"I did? Oh, yes." He looked at her, puzzled, then he flushed, guilty that he had forgotten the only letter he had ever sent her.

"It's best to forget everything connected with times like that," she said quickly. "What about your grandson? David?"

"Yes, David. He's fine. I saw him and his aunt yesterday morning. I judged some trials in San Francisco last week."

"Oh? And I'll bet David was proud of his grandpa!"

"I couldn't say." Cappy shrugged. "He didn't come to the field, had other things to do." He studied his plate, moved a potato with his fork, then added, "I suppose Nadine arranged the other things. She knows I never liked her sister, and doesn't forgive me for it. It doesn't matter. The boy and I haven't anything in common. He's more like Alice, his mother, than like Ben."

"Why, Cappy! You sound as though you have something against the boy."

"Oh, I don't dislike him," he said. "I quarreled with Ben about his marriage—you know that. I expected him to finish medical school, wanted him to bring a wife home one day—a wife who'd fit into the plans Ben and I made for Rancho San Pascual. Well, Alice changed everything, and I was bitter. I don't hold that against David, of course. Although I admit he doesn't seem to have much backbone. Mostly I just don't know him, and it's too late to get acquainted now. Better leave things alone."

"Too late? It's never too late for anything important." He had violated an article of her faith and her protest was strong.

"Suit yourself," he said. "Is there any pie?"

"Yes, cherry."

She brought a wedge of pie and took away the dirty dishes. The screen door banged twice in the rising wind and she bolted it, then joined him again.

"Now tell me about your real family. I mean the four-footed ones," she said, chuckling. "Last time you had a beautiful puppy with you—I remember the silver in his coat. You thought too much silver. You called him Starfall."

"Yes. Starfall." Cappy avoided her eyes. "He turned out fine, not too much silver."

"I suppose he's winning all kinds of ribbons and siring puppies you're selling for a fortune."

"Yes, he did well, a fine guard. Two daughters are seeing-eyes," Cappy could not quite conceal the catch in his voice. "They've *all* done well. Things have never been better." He turned his head, pretended to listen to the rain.

"Cappy, what happened?" Her voice was sharp and she leaned toward him. "Something's wrong. I hear it in your voice, I feel it. Tell me!"

He had not intended to talk about what had happened, had meant to pretend that all was well with him. At least he believed this had been his intention. Yet why had he come here if not to unburden himself? In the last six months he had talked to no one about his loss, but never put his grief into words. He was a man who lived only with himself and the thought that anyone might pity him was unendurable. Nor did he believe anyone else could comprehend the tragedy that had befallen him. Yet, feeling the warmth of Miss Myrna's hand resting lightly on his, he was able for the first time to talk about what had happened.

"They're gone, all of them. Dead, destroyed. Fourteen German Shepherds as beautiful as God ever created. The work of a lifetime—wiped out in an hour. Just . . . gone. I still can't believe it."

He spoke quietly with almost no emotion in his voice, but a vein in his left temple pulsed and his jaw had a hard, tense set.

"It started with such a little, unimportant thing. Something went wrong with the drains in the kennel runs. Water was backing up and flooding. So I moved the dogs into the old barn I built years ago when Ben and I had horses. It was warm and dry—I really didn't think much about it since they'd only be there a couple of days.

"I had this lovely bitch, Shenandoah. She'd had her second litter by Starfall, and—oh—those five puppies were beautiful. I was keeping one, a little pixie called Star Shadow. I'd sold the other four by mail, and that morning I was driving to the city to ship them at the airport to their new homes. And I was also shipping Blaze to David in San Francisco. Blaze was from a different whelping, seven pups I called my 'fire litter,' because they all had such flash and sparkle. Blaze was the first of them to leave. The fire litter! What a gruesome joke that turned into!" Closing his eyes, he drew a long breath.

"Blaze?" she asked.

"Yes, my final problem. I'll tell you later." He shook his head, then went on with his story. "So I took the five puppies in sky crates and drove three hours to the airport. Everything went wrong and it was almost dark when the last pup got off. I was tired and decided to stay in the city that night. There was no reason for worry. Mrs. Littlefoot—she's my housekeeper—and her nephew would take care of things at home."

Cappy paused, looked at the rain streaming down the windows. "It was five minutes after three—I looked at my watch—when the phone rang in my hotel room. It was Mrs. Littlefoot, sobbing and mumbling, but I finally understood her. The stable had somehow caught fire. It was gone in ten minutes, burned like a matchbox. The floor and walls were brick, so I'd never thought of fire. I never thought about the shingle roof and the rafters and wooden stalls and loft."

He leaned against the booth, closing his eyes. "They were trapped inside, all of them. Starfall and Shenandoah and the six pups. Cheyenne was killed, so was my beautiful Astrid and Lancer ... and all the others. Gone ... all gone."

His voice trailed to silence, and he sat motionless with closed eyes, resting his forehead on his hands as he listened to the downpour of rain. But he also heard the roar of the burning stable, the cries of trapped animals. No one on earth could imagine what he felt when he saw the embers, still smoking and sparking in the pale dawn. These were the charred ruins of his life, so long to build, so fast to vanish.

Miss Myrna allowed him his moments of grief, then said, "So what have you done since? How are you starting over?"

"Starting over?" He stared at her. "There's no way to start. Everything's finished. I'm finished."

He could not explain to her that beginning again was not a simple matter of buying new breeding stock, finding puppies descended from German Shepherds he himself had bred and others with similar qualities and characters. The animals that had perished were the culmination of generations of work, not just good Shepherds, but *his* good Shepherds. Even if he were allowed time to recreate them, he felt too bitter, too tired.

Impulsively Miss Myrna took his hand, opened the closed fingers. She did not look at his palm, but felt the ridges and creases.

"No, there's no future to read," he told her.

Her eyes seemed strangely bright, their gaze intent upon him. "There will be love and happiness you have not expected, but you must not be afraid to take what comes."

Gently he withdrew his hand. "Thank you, Gypsy," he said. "You don't see the journey I'm making tomorrow? Or money or a dark lady?"

"I've told you what I saw, and the dark lady has no part in it. You will not meet her again, I think. But you should listen to her."

Rising, she moved to the screen door, stood staring across the driveway past the lonely, solitary gas pump into the night. "Do you hear the water rising in the arroyo? It was dry an hour ago, but it'll be a torrent by morning."

"I hear it."

"Now, when it's raining, you can see how that dry bed turns into a river. But I've watched it in the dry seasons. Bone-dry days when that whole world out there is dead dust and nothing can live there, not one blade of grass.

"There won't be a cloud in that blazing sky. But suddenly the water comes and rises, the arroyo banks turn green. There's life again."

"I suppose that means rain in the mountains," Cappy said. "Clouds too far away to be seen."

She nodded. "I think that's how everything begins for us. We can't see things until they come—like the water."

"I should have known you had a faith like that."

She turned from the doorway, smiling. "Of course. Faith is God's cheapest favor." Miss Myrna tilted her head toward the parking area. "How good to see your van out there again. But it's strange to think that for once there aren't any dogs in it."

"But there is a dog. Blaze, the pup I sent David. I'm taking him back."

"Taking back your grandson's pup? Why, Cappy!"

"He didn't keep it," said the old man gruffly. "His aunt doesn't like dogs, and I suppose David didn't stand up to her."

"Well, then you'll still have one dog at the ranch." She looked relieved and smiled.

"I won't keep him except long enough to find out if it's safe to turn him over to someone else." Cappy frowned. "Poor Blaze! Too dangerous to keep and too beautiful to destroy."

"Maybe he just needs someone to give him love."

"Sure." Cappy lifted an eyebrow. "That's what we all need."

"You're wrong, you know," she told him. "We need to give love, but it doesn't much matter if we get any back." Miss Myrna took away his empty pie plate. "So you'll sort of test this Blaze, and if he passes, you'll give him away?"

"Give him away?" Cappy looked shocked. "Great God, no! I'll sell him. *Never* give a dog away. People don't respect things they don't pay for. Blaze was the first dog I gave anybody—except one to Ben long ago—and look what happened. Most of the abused, mistreated dogs in the world were once somebody's loving gift!" He saw his vehemence had startled her, so he smiled quickly and said, "Would you like to see Blaze?"

"Yes, very much."

"All right. Just as soon as I've had some coffee and the rain stops."

"Fine," she said, going to the big metal urn and picking up a mug. "There's no hurry."

David, huddled against the wall of the van, felt a new surge of fear as he realized that the dog's eyes were now fully open and watching him.

The interior was so dark that he could see only vague shapes and outlines, but a beam from the driveway lights entered the window from the cab, making a pale gray patch on the floor where the dog rested his head on his heavy paws. Above the black muzzle and glint of white teeth David could discern a gleam of the open eyes. No white was visible, only two unwavering reflections of deep gold revealed that Blaze had awakened again, that the tranquilizing drug was rapidly losing its effect.

Blaze hardly stirred—an ear flicked and once his coat seemed to rustle in a slight shiver—yet David sensed that the animal was troubled, deeply uneasy, but he could not imagine the silent conflicts beginning to arouse the dog's lulled but awakening emotions. Blaze knew for certain that here was one of the miniature people who had tormented him in the past, an enemy to be attacked and destroyed.

It was his nature, bred into him through countless generations, to protect his territory, which the van had become, to drive off and if necessary destroy intruders. To attack was a duty and a compulsion. Still, another voice, although it was almost stilled by what he had suffered, whispered that this creature was one of those special beings toward whom he owed gentleness and protection. This feeling was also an emotion of his breed, instilled in his blood. So he did not know what to do, and lay quietly, waiting for some sign, some unknown prompting.

So the dog and the boy watched each other, neither moving, both on guard for the first signal from his enemy.

When Cappy had left, locking the van behind him, David had not realized for a moment that Blaze was no longer locked in his cage. Then, with fear like a cold shock, he heard the animal pacing and snuffling near the rear door. David held his breath, squeezing into the corner behind the burlap curtain, making himself as small as possible, so small he thought he might become invisible. He wondered if there were some magic through whose power he could shrink until he vanished.

He knew he had no such power, that Blaze was fearfully real and would not disappear in smoke or melt like a lemon drop. Yet, although he knew better, David's mind reached toward escapes that were magical. He had heard Cappy say that dogs loved to be talked to, he remembered his grandfather's strange singing, the reciting of poems and things from the Bible.

He remembered a story a nurse had read him about a boy and a princess who had held a horde of evil goblins at bay by reciting verses, and as long as they kept saying rhymes, the goblins could not attack. Could it be the same with Blaze? If he talked and showed no fear, would he then be safe? But he was afraid to speak, afraid to make the least sound.

Minutes and more minutes passed, an eternity, then the dog seemed to sleep, his breathing deep and even. Edging the curtain aside, David peered cautiously at Blaze. He felt terribly afraid of the dog, and from all that Cappy had said, he knew how dangerous the animal could be. Last night, when he had slipped past the cage to go outside the van, he had heard for himself the savagery of Blaze's attack upon the locked door.

But mixed with this fear, David harbored a strange wonder and fascination, an almost desperate longing for the dog to like him. Earlier today, looking from behind the curtain, he had seen Blaze racing and bounding in the desert meadow—the freest, the most beautiful animal David had ever seen. He had marveled at the power and pure joy of running, and he thought that even he himself could run like that if only Blaze ran beside him.

And, after all, Blaze was *his* dog, belonged to him. Blaze should love him. They were going together into the unknown, he and Blaze. They should be companions and friends.

Yet he knew better. Abandoning his dream, he forced his eyes to search the dark for a safer place or even a weapon. He remembered there was a tool box near the door, but realized he could never tiptoe past the dog to reach it. Even if he had some weapon, a wrench or a tire tool, Blaze was many times his strength. David would be knocked to the floor by the first lunge; he was defenseless and he knew it. Somehow he stopped himself from screaming.

The rain that had been hammering the roof of the truck slackened, and now its monotonous patter seemed to lull the dog until eventually his eyes closed again. A moment later his paws jerked and twitched in fitful sleep, a dream of pursuit and capture, while David still looked for a better hiding place.

Near the ceiling was a narrow wooden shelf, and if he could reach it by climbing on top of the cupboard, then squeezed back, would he be out of reach? How high could the dog jump?

David edged forward silently, the burlap brushing roughly against his face. Steadying himself, he put his hand on the top of the cupboard, just outside the curtain, then gasped as his fingers touched an empty tin cup, which slipped on the smooth wood and fell to the floor with a clatter. Suddenly, terrifyingly the dog growled—a lower and different sound than David had heard before.

David's mouth went dry, his heart pounded as he tried to remember what his grandfather had said. "They want you to talk, they like to hear your voice ... The words don't matter ..."

He would talk to Blaze, make him know he was a friend. Blaze *had* to understand. *Please, Blaze, don't hurt me!*

David drew himself into a ball behind the curtain, closing his eyes tight, trembling as he waited. The growl became a snarl, then David again forced back a scream as the van echoed with furious barking. His eyes snapped open when without warning the burlap was ripped from its rod. Blazed slashed the cloth with his teeth, rending it, then hurled the tattered curtain aside to turn to face his human enemy.

David, dodging away from the knifelike teeth, had instinctively leaped from the cupboard and stood with his back to the screened window of the cab, arms outstretched against the wall as though pinned there. He did not think

he could speak, could make a sound, then his voice came
to him, a quivering tremolo, and he forced out the words.

"Blaze ... Now there, Blaze. You won't hurt me, will
you, Blaze? Remember, I'm David ... We're friends,
Blaze, friends ..."

Cappy finished his coffee and stood up. "Rain's stopped.
It's time I let that ruffian out for some air, so if you want
to see him, come along."

She looked doubtful. "Maybe I'd be safer seeing him
through the window. Can't you bring him up here?"

"You can sit in the cab. I don't want him getting wind
of that pack of varments you keep. He might want to
swallow three or four, and I'd never get either of you quiet
again. Are they locked in?"

"Yes, in the back."

She touched a switch and an extra floodlight brilliantly
illuminated the parking area where the van stood some
distance away.

"Don't expect a show or a field trial," he warned her.
"I've been feeding him and he's used to me. But I
wouldn't want to try to manage this fellow very far. He
might turn into a timber wolf."

She chuckled. "You used to say you could handle anything with four feet and a bark."

"Still can. But I'm not pushing my luck."

They strolled toward the van, following a zigzag route
to avoid puddles of rainwater in the thin gravel. "Still the
same truck?" She squinted ahead. "I recognize the sunflowers."

"Yes. Ben painted those crazy flowers the last summer he was home. Not much left of them now."

They were approaching the van from the rear. Cappy lifted his head rather sharply when he heard furious barking erupt inside. "Well, my friend seems to be on guard."

Miss Myrna did not notice the uncertainty in his voice. "Lord, he sounds like a lion attacking something in there!" Her shoulders imitated a shiver. "Cappy, has anybody ever opened the door by accident when you had a guard dog in there?"

"No. I'm careful about locking up. Wouldn't matter much anyway. All my dogs—until this one—were trained to guard the van, not jump out of it. But everybody who handles or shows big dogs has a nightmare about a child opening the wrong cage or putting his hand in. Funny, in all these years I've never known that to happen—but everybody still has the nightmare."

Cappy's mind was not really on what he was saying. He was still pondering things Miss Myrna had told him in the last hour, thoughts that disturbed him. Yet because he had spent his life near animals and knew their moods, something in Blaze's barking seemed wrong to him. Dogs did not merely bark: they called, greeted, requested, complained, and applauded. Then there was the whole lexicon of warnings, ranging from token challenges to the ferocious threats Cappy called "business barks." It struck him now that the barking he heard meant dangerous business, and he wondered if some animal had approached the van, perhaps taken shelter under it.

Then he heard a snarl, not a deep guttural warning, but

high in the throat, a rasp that was the last threat before attack. Cappy quickly handed Miss Myrna a key from his ring. "Get in the cab and close the door. I want to talk to this fellow before we're face to face. Something—God knows what—has made him hysterical."

Then Cappy halted, eyes wide, a look of unbelief on this face. Faintly but unmistakably he heard a high-pitched voice, a child's voice, speaking inside the van. The wooden wall muffled all the words except "Blaze," which was repeated again and again.

Cappy rushed toward the door, realizing that somehow the impossible and unthinkable had happened, the nightmare about a child had come true. As he unfastened the padlock, he did not even wonder how such a thing had taken place, he only knew that it had.

As he dropped the padlock to the ground, he was so close to panic that he almost yielded to his impulse to fling the door open without losing a second. But he realized in time that any alarming move could prove fatal, he could very well end up lying on his back in the gravel, the dog on top of him, slashing. He rattled the door handle loudly, then waited a second or two before speaking.

"Blaze, Blaze, old fellow," he called, clearly but not shouting. "What's the matter? I've come back, so it's all right now. Easy, Blaze, just take it easy now."

The silence in the van seemed ominous. He eased the door open slowly, an inch at a time, bracing himself in case the dog hurled his weight against the panel. No lunge came, instead he heard once more the danger-growl signaling attack.

Slowly but steadily Cappy opened the door. The dog, angrily wheeling back and forth in the narrow aisle, seemed hardly aware of Cappy. His attention was riveted on a small prisoner he had cornered against the cab. The little boy's face lay hidden in shadow, and Cappy had no suspicion that this could be his grandson. He only knew that in an inconceivable manner a child had broken into the van and that Blaze, still utterly out of control, was deadly.

"You there, son! Don't move a finger." He spoke in the same calm, cheerful tone he used to the dog and kept all fear out of his voice. "Blaze! Hey, Blaze!"

Ignoring Cappy, the dog stopped his frenzied pacing and lowered his body to a crouch, ready to spring, his tail lashing.

If only, Cappy thought, he had a gun in his hand. He had never killed a dog, but now he would have fired with no hesitation. Yet, before throwing himself bodily upon the animal, he made one desperate try with words.

"You now, Blaze!" he shouted, clapping his hands sharply. The dog half turned his head, realized Cappy was there.

"The Camptown ladies sing this song, doo-dah, doo-dah . . ."

Cappy sang lustily. Memory of all other songs, even of this one, had gone completely from his head, and he sang without any real tune or words, holding his hands at his shoulders and snapping his fingers lightly. *"Oh, Blaze is a dog that's five miles long . . . something, something . . ."*

Cappy's hand drifted to his shirt pocket, searching for the liver bait he carried there, then he remembered it was inside the cab. But on the floor, near the door of the van, sat Blaze's empty food dish. Cappy picked it up carefully, tapped it against the cage.

"Blaze, come on now, boy. See what I've got for you."

The dog stood quietly, then turned toward him, confused, unwilling to give up his attack, yet fascinated by Cappy.

"Oh we can't wait all night, we can't wait all day,
Blaze, boy! Blaze, boy! . . ."

Slowly the dog came toward him, hesitating once, casting back a look and growling. Cappy extended his hand, holding it lower than the dog's muzzle and with the palm upward. When Blaze reached him, he gently scratched the dog's chest while with the other hand he pushed the food dish far into the open cage.

"Go on, Blaze. Time for bed, in you go. Now that's a good boy!"

He cajoled the dog with his voice and his hands, urging him on with gentleness. And Blaze, assured by Cappy's manner and easy touch, went peacefully into the cage, turned around twice, and lay down comfortably while Cappy latched the door.

"Oh, thank God, thank God!" exclaimed Miss Myrna, and for the first time Cappy realized she had been watching just behind him, a large rock in each hand.

The boy in the van took a step forward, started to speak, then swayed as though about to crumple to the floor.

"David! Oh, God, David! How—?" Cappy lifted the boy in his arms, carried him from the van, David's body seeming surprisingly frail and thin. Bewildered, Cappy said to Miss Myrna, "It's David, Ben's boy. I didn't know—oh!"

"Take him inside, Cappy," she said. "Come now, don't just stand there. It's starting to rain." She snapped the padlock on the door of the van.

As they started toward the lunchroom, David looked up at Cappy, his dark eyes big, and spoke in a whisper. "I wasn't much afraid of him. Just tired of standing there—but I wasn't afraid. Blaze wouldn't really bite me."

Cappy, still dazed, did not answer, but Miss Myrna patted David's hand. "Of course, you weren't afraid, anyone could see that. Neither one of you. I think I've just seen the two bravest fellows anywhere. For a fact, I have!"

Cappy, without realizing it, held David closer. "You've been in there all the way from San Francisco?" Cappy asked.

"Yes."

"Why didn't you tell me you were there?"

"I was afraid of you."

"I see. Not afraid of Blaze, but afraid of me?" To Cappy's surprise the boy nodded.

"Why did you run away, David? Why?"

"I don't know." His eyes evaded Cappy's, and he seemed then to search for the answer to a riddle. "Maybe I just came to be with my dog."

"No more questions tonight," said Miss Myrna. "Some hot food and a good bed for this young man. But no more questions."

An hour later Cappy was slowly pacing the floor of the lunchroom when Miss Myrna returned from putting David to bed in one of the cabins.

"You were gone a long time," said Cappy. "Did he talk to you?"

"Yes." She smiled. "Young or old, men always talk to me. You can forget driving down to the junction to phone his aunt. She thinks he's at some camp and she's away for two or three weeks herself, so no one's worried."

Miss Myrna put on her glasses and, sitting at the counter, began to deal and redeal a worn pack of cards, turning up three at a time and placing them in a star-shaped design. "Your grandson's as stubborn as you are. Scared as he was, he wanted to go back to the van and talk to Blaze—to show there weren't any hard feelings."

"Well, that's one idea of his that makes sense. Just what he ought to do, except they've both had too much excitement." Cappy sat on the stool next to Miss Myrna.

"The cards tell me something," she said, lifting an eyebrow. "It says here that in a very little while a certain little boy is going to slip out of his room and say good night to that dog."

"Just let me catch him trying it! He's done his share of mischief for the year!"

"No, Cappy. Let him do it if he wants to. There's no harm. It's sort of like getting back on a horse after you've fallen, isn't it?"

"Well, he ought to ask permission," said Cappy gruffly.

"Permission to do a wise thing?"

Cappy shrugged. "All right. Did he tell you why he stowed away in the van? Damn fool stunt!"

"But he already said why." She began gathering the cards.

"You mean to be with the dog? Huh! He didn't even know what he meant then."

"Maybe he thought it was a reason you'd like to hear, a reason you'd understand. And it is, isn't it?"

Cappy turned away from her, sudden color showing beneath the deep tan of his cheeks. "What the devil do you mean? That's ridiculous."

"He told me he was going with you to the ranch—that he and Blaze were going to live there."

"*What?* His aunt'd never allow it. Besides, I've forgotten anything I ever knew about little boys and I don't intend to learn again."

"Oh, I think they're something like your German Shepherds. If you give them enough care and patience, they turn out fairly well." Taking his hands in hers, she held them tightly. "Keep him as long as you can, Cappy. I'm right, I know about these things, believe me!"

He shook his head. "Once I talk to his aunt, back he goes! But right now I don't seem to have much choice."

Miss Myrna rose, switched off the floodlights, the neon sign, and the fluorescent tubes in the lunchroom, leaving only a night lamp above the cash register. "You'll leave early in the morning?"

"Yes. We'll say good-bye then."

"No, I'll be asleep. You come in the back door and get your own breakfast—and the boy's, of course."

"The boy's? Cook *his* breakfast?" Cappy's face was a portrait of shock. "Not on your life! Next you'll tell me to change his diapers!"

"I doubt that'll be necessary," she retorted, "but you

might remember that *somebody* once changed yours." She returned her glasses to her apron pocket. "Oh, Cappy, I love seeing you walk in that door. But I could never stand farewells, never. So go along in the morning and don't bother me."

He stepped close and kissed her.

From the rear of the building came a sharp barking muffled by a closed door. Miss Myrna turned toward the window. "Listen, someone's crossing the gravel, the dogs always know."

"It's David. He's slipped out of his cabin, just as you predicted." Cappy took a step toward the door, then stopped. "Well, as you say, no harm done."

A moment later Blaze sounded a loud warning in the van. "We'll have an hour of this now," grumbled Cappy. "I told you so."

"I suppose you've never heard a dog bark at night before?" Then she laid her hand on Cappy's arm. "Be gentle with him."

"Of course. Did you ever know me to be less than gentle with any dog?"

She laughed, shaking her head. "Oh, what an outrageous grandfather you are! I didn't mean the dog, I meant David."

"Well ... uh ... yes. I suppose I won't do him any great damage in the next day or two."

A cloud moved westward revealing the moon and in the faint light Cappy could just distinguish a small figure in polka dot pajamas standing near the van. He sighed, wrinkling his brow. A ridiculous situation, Cappy thought, and he resolved to bounce the boy back to San Francisco at the first airport.

Yet at the same time, watching now and remembering David standing so silent, so unflinching before the raging dog, Cappy felt an unfamiliar emotion, almost a wistfulness, though it was not sadness but contentment, a feeling he had known before, so long ago he could not remember when.

"You know, what he did tonight took some courage."

Miss Myrna glanced at him. "Yes. Do you suppose it comes from good blood lines?"

Four

Cappy awakened at dawn, fresh and vigorous, eager to
be on his way, feeling sure that his visit here was over. It
was always the same—he was happy to arrive here, grateful
for what he found, and content in leaving.

He shaved carefully around the edges of his beard, and
found himself humming. The face in the mirror seemed a
little different today, even a little younger—which was
foolishness. It was unusual for him to notice such a thing,
for he took himself for granted and had no vanity about
his appearance except for being scrupulously neat and
scrubbed clean.

At six o'clock he decided it was time to rout David
from his bed in the next cabin, and as he put on his cap
and strapped on his watch, he mentally outlined a brief,
snappy admonition about seizing the day and about the re-
wards for the early worm.

But this good advice was never delivered, because he
found David already dressed and waiting on the step outside his own cabin.

"I thought we'd want to start early so we could get home tonight," said David cheerfully.

Home? Cappy shook his head. "With that antique I'm driving, I'll be lucky to see Rancho San Pascual by tomorrow afternoon. Now the back door of the restaurant's unlocked, so you go find yourself something to eat. I'll be along shortly—when it comes to getting breakfast, it's every man for himself," he said sternly, fixing David with an eye that would bar all questions. "I'm going down to the van to clean the cage and feed Blaze."

"Feed him? How often does he eat?"

"He only needs one meal a day. I'm feeding him two or three times because it's a way for us to get better acquainted."

"Can I come along and help?"

"Not this time. I'm in a hurry."

David nodded, hid his disappointment. "Okay. Then I'll go get breakfast, Grandpa."

Cappy winced. "Hold it right there! David, I want you to understand this clearly. By blood and law I'm your grandfather, it's true. But I am *nobody's* grandpa. My name is Cappy. You remember that."

"Yes, Cappy. Yes, sir!" David gave a sharp little military salute, about-faced, and headed toward the restaurant, while Cappy watched him uncertainly, not sure how to take this last joke.

Blaze was in a playful, puppyish mood, all traces of last night's anger having vanished. Cappy let the dog run free, trusting that no strange animals would wander near. The dog returned willingly to a clean cage, and Cappy went to the lunchroom, thinking not very happily about day-old doughnuts and canned fruit juice.

David was waiting for him. "I've scrambled some eggs for you, Cappy, and made toast and squeezed oranges. There's bacon, but I'm not good at frying it. I'm still learning about bacon."

"How did you learn to scramble eggs?"

"Aunt Nadine hates to get up early when Uncle Arthur isn't home. I take care of myself." He looked Cappy in the eye.

Cappy nodded. "Good eggs. A lot better than I can make."

David washed the dishes while Cappy wrote an awkward note to Miss Myrna, ending as he always ended such notes with "See you soon," and wondering if he would. He left the note on the counter, then put money in the open cash register for their food and lodging.

As they walked toward the van, Cappy noticed that the water in the arroyo had vanished, but all along its sides there were pale green shoots, tiny new life struggling to grow. Turning back, he waved good-bye to the little cluster of desolate buildings and their owner. Miss Myrna, he felt, had again given him something, although he was not sure what the gift had been.

A few hours later they were crossing the Arizona Plateau.

Cappy had tried twice to telephone Nadine in San Francisco, but there had been no answer.

"I told you, Cappy. She's away. She and Uncle Arthur

won't be home for weeks." The boy had not let Cappy know why they were away, and had evaded all questions about his own flight from home.

"You know it's not right your running off like this," said Cappy. "The people at that camp where you should have gone must be terribly worried. At the next town I'll call them. What did you say the name of the camp was?"

"I didn't say." David, who sat with his legs folded under him, turned in his seat. "Cappy, are you planning to put me on a plane in Flagstaff and try to send me to the camp?"

"Well, I suppose that's the only right thing to do," said Cappy, uncomfortable that his half-formed scheme had been anticipated. "Now, David, if you had *asked* ahead to come with me, instead of running off—"

"You wouldn't have let me come," David said simply.

"Here now, son! Of course I would have."

"For sure, Cappy? Are you talking honest?"

Cappy hesitated, swallowed. "Not honest, David. I wouldn't have let you come."

They rode for a while in silence, avoiding each other's eyes, David looking out the side window, Cappy staring straight ahead, feeling guilty at having been caught in a lie and at the same time, for no sensible reason, remembering Miss Myrna's telling of his fortune.

Blaze, sensitive to the change of mood, stirred in his cage, then gave a questioning bark.

"Blaze understands us," said David.

Cappy shrugged. "Well, maybe he understands us as well as we understand one another."

David began to sing softly. It was the almost tuneless song Cappy had sung to Blaze yesterday, but David remembered his father humming it as he drove his car.

"O'er the measureless range
Where seldom change
The swart gray plains
So weird and strange . . ."

To Cappy, listening, the scene felt strangely natural and at the same time impossible. He might have been driving to a dog show or, more likely, an obedience trial. Ben might have been sitting beside him, crooning in a boyish soprano, off key just as David was. And behind them in the van, or in earlier vans, rode the proud German Shepherd Dogs. Not just the few they might be hauling to Albuquerque or Denver, or the herding dogs they delivered to the great sheep ranches in Nevada and Utah. Not only those, for the van, in Cappy's imagination, grew long as a train behind them and the train was filled with all the animals of his life.

"All right, David," he said, turning the truck into the drive of a gasoline station. "Tell me the name of the camp. I won't send you there, but I have to phone them."

"You promise?" David's eyes were suspicious.

"Don't ask a damn fool question. When I tell you I'm going to do something or not do it, it's *always* a promise. And you make certain it's the same way when you talk. Clear?"

"Clear, Cappy." From his pocket he took a crumpled

piece of paper. "Here's the number. And I'll bet it's a rotten outfit."

It was almost dusk when they left the highway and took a winding dirt road that eventually brought them to a hacienda where they were to spend the night. This was Navajo country, and although the ranch and its ten thousand sheep were not part of a reservation, the owner and his wife and many children looked exactly like the Navajo people David had seen along the roads and in the little towns during the last two hours.

The family greeted Cappy with warmth but there was a shyness in their smiles. Few visitors came to this hidden place, and they saw unknown faces only on their rare visits to town. David could not understand their language, and felt disappointed when Cappy told him they were speaking Spanish. He had hoped it was Navajo.

Cappy exercised Blaze in the sunset light, which made his coat shine with an auburn glow. Cappy took David by the hand and led him close to Blaze. "Don't be afraid. He sees you as part of me now, and knows it's all right."

"I'm not afraid anyhow." David forced himself not to tremble.

The ranch family crowded the windows of the house to watch Blaze run, exclaiming at the dog's strength and speed. David, although he could not make out the words, swelled with pride and later tried to explain to a boy his own age that he was Blaze's owner. The boy seemed delighted by David's gestures, but there was no look of understanding in his face.

After Blaze was safely locked away, Senor Ortiz, the ranch owner, brought from a barn two ancient, tottering German Shepherd Dogs who could no longer recognize Cappy by sound or sight, but upon sniffing him, set up a joyful clamor. They capered on stiff joints, painfully shouldering each other out of the way in jealous bids to be petted. A quarrelsome old couple who had grown crotchety together, they could not quite stop bickering and snapping even in the presence of a favorite caller.

"Both twelve years old and trying to frisk like puppies again!" exclaimed Cappy, both his hands buried in fur as he scratched their chests.

"Is twelve very old?" David asked.

"Yes. This pair retired from work just two years ago, but until then, they were two of the best sheepherders I ever bred. There's a narrow bridge across a stream back there a mile or so." Cappy gestured to the north. "These two could funnel a herd across it faster than any five men. I met Senor Ortiz when I sold him these dogs as pups."

Cappy pressed David's hands on the hindquarters of the male. "Feel those muscles, David. That's a *working* dog, even at his age. A good sheep dog covers about fifty miles a day in fertile country. A lot more than that on this ranch."

That night they slept on narrow beds with woven ropes for springs and straw ticks for mattresses. The ticks had a faint smell of clover.

"Crazy beds!" said David.

"Crazy? I've slept on a bed like this all my life, and your father was born in one."

Just as he was falling asleep, David heard a faraway howling sound, then from another direction an answer.

"Wolves, Cappy?" he asked, snuggling comfortably.

"No. Just two sheep dogs in different meadows miles away. They're having a talk, telling each other where they are. When the moon sets or goes behind a cloud, they'll say good night." And they did.

In the morning Cappy and David were again up with the sun and driving into the clear morning toward distant peaks tipped with snow, reminding David of the white world and his father, but these thoughts were pushed aside by excitement as each hour brought them closer and closer to Rancho San Pascual.

"Why does it have that funny name? San Pascual?"

"Because in this part of the world a saint called San Pascual protects sheep and shepherds."

"I see. And the dogs from San Pascual were mostly dogs for sheep herding?"

"No, only some of them. German Shepherd Dogs herd sheep naturally, and there aren't any better herders in the world. But some ranchers want smaller dogs that are cheaper to feed, or they have very small flocks and can't buy the best dogs. Mostly I bred puppies for pets and for guide dogs for the blind and for use as guards."

They drove on, skirting the suburbs of a city. "Over there's the airport," said Cappy firmly. "It's from there you'll take off for San Francisco one day before long."

David, seeming not to hear, glanced over his shoulder. "Blaze is quieter today," he said.

The village lay at the foot of a mountain and a map of it would have resembled a tic-tac-toe game, four straight streets intersecting to form a square in the middle. A mission church faced this plaza and so did the general store, a saloon, the post office, a two-story brick barn that was the feed store and also the tallest building except for the belfry of the church. Now in the late afternoon the half dozen other commercial enterprises seemed to be asleep and, indeed, were never very wakeful. It was a poor town, but a modestly pretty one, the inhabitants unembarrassed that the geraniums on the window sills were potted in tin coffee cans or that chickens roamed at large in the streets. Tall, stiff hollyhocks stood behind fences that at one time or another had been whitewashed.

Cappy drove slowly past the plaza, a square of grass thinly shaded by drooping junipers. He nodded to passersby and saluted the elderly men in broad-brimmed hats and high-heeled boots who lounged on the porch of the Hotel Hacienda, which was also called Mrs. Christie's boardinghouse.

When they left the town and the foothills, the truck wheezed as the road climbed toward aspen forest on the southern ridge of the great mountain. There seemed to be no breeze, yet the aspen leaves trembled, and this, as everyone in the village and the canyon knew, was because the True Cross was made of aspen trunks and ever since the repentant trees have quaked and trembled.

After circling the ridge they entered a canyon where a narrow stream foamed white against gray boulders.

"Cappy, how did anybody ever find the way here to buy a puppy?"

Cappy raised an eyebrow. "Not too many did. Lucky I had a pension, wasn't it?" Then he chuckled. "I shipped more dogs to New York City than I ever sold in this state. San Pascual Shepherds went everywhere—for police departments, for guiding the blind, rescue dogs to work in mountains like these where people might get lost."

The canyon gradually broadened and softened into a green valley with scattered stands of pine and spruce. Between the groves stretched winding meadows tall with grass. Then, on the right and almost at the edge of the road, rose a high stone wall, an impressive work of masonry, its dark mortar still glossy with newness. As they passed big double gates of lacy ironwork, David glimpsed a lawn surrounding a swimming pool and beyond it a landscaped garden. A small sign above the gate said, "Spirit Canyon Lodge."

"A hotel?" David asked.

"No, just an expensive new house with a fancy name. A rich widow from the city built it this year."

A jeep was approaching from the opposite direction, and Cappy pulled aside in the shadow of the wall to let the vehicle pass on the narrow road. "And this is the same lady," said Cappy without enthusiasm.

Instead of passing, the jeep pulled up beside them. "Oh, Captain Holland," a woman's voice twittered, "do wait just a minute!"

David stared first at the jeep, which was decorated with pink fringe and plastic daisies, then at its two occupants, who impressed him as being extraordinary. The man at the wheel was sallow faced and dark haired. Everything about him, David thought, was narrow or thin—his mustache looked like two single slashes from a black crayon, and so did his eyebrows, which were set above hawk's eyes in a hawklike face. A slender hand with tapering fingers rested elegantly on the windowless door of the jeep, the wrist tightly encased in the French cuff of a gray silk shirt. The hand glittered—links, watch, and a ring winking like diamonds in the sun.

The woman in the passenger's seat wore a sun hat so enormous that she appeared to be hiding beneath it, and David thought of an elf lurking under a giant toadstool. Her hair, cascading in ashen waves below her shoulders, shone like the spun glass used to decorate Christmas trees in department stores. Beneath the coatings of makeup she had a rather pretty, doll-like face, David decided. He had no idea of her age, but it had to be far from young.

"Well, Captain Holland, how nice to see you back! I hear you've been on the West Coast piling up some kind of honors," she cried.

"Good afternoon, Mrs. Bradley." Cappy nodded politely, touching the bill of his cap.

"I suppose you've met Carlos Jones?" she asked, indicating the driver.

"I have." Cappy looked at the man, his face like flint. Jones muttered an inaudible greeting, then became preoccupied with the inspection of his own fingernails.

Seeming unaware of the animosity between the two men, Mrs. Bradley rattled on. "Carlos has been helping me find stones for my little Japanese garden. We discovered remarkable ones at a place—what's it called? Rim Rock Trail?"

"That's a dangerous road and a dangerous area," said Cappy. "I advise you to stay away from there."

"Now don't scold me, Captain Holland!" She took off her harlequin sunglasses and waggled the frames at Cappy. "A week from Sunday I'm having a housewarming for the Lodge. Cocktails and lunch. I've sent you an invitation, of course. A swarm of people from the state capital will be here, but I'd feel just devastated if my nearest neighbor didn't attend. You will come, won't you?" Tilting her head, she coaxed him with her smile.

"I will remember the date," said Cappy.

"Oh, good!" she exclaimed, not noticing his evasion. "I've had a feeling that you're positively antisocial at times, Captain, and I do hope it's not personal with me because I'm such a cat fancier."

"Loving dogs doesn't preclude loving cats, Mrs. Bradley. I'm fond of almost all animals."

"Then I must show you Flossie!" Reaching below the seat, Mrs. Bradley seemed to tussle with something, then lifted up a great bundle of white fluff that straightened itself into the shape of a very plump and very irritable Persian cat.

"Isn't she gorgeous! Flossie-wossie!"

The cat glared at Cappy, its eyes full of pure hate. "Phsst!" it hissed, white fur bristling. Carlos Jones cringed, sinking more deeply into the driver's seat.

"I have six of them now, and Flossie's the prettiest." She waved the animal proudly.

Suddenly Blaze, catching a scent, burst into enraged barking, leaping forward to clatter the metal door, then banging against the wooden panel. Mrs. Bradley's smile dissolved.

"A dog?" she shouted above the noise.

Cappy nodded gravely, and Mrs. Bradley thrust the spitting Persian into concealment on the floor of the jeep.

Carlos Jones now seemed to take an interest in the van, leaning out as though he hoped to see the author of such a savage racket. For an instant Jones's eyes and Cappy's met, then Jones looked away.

"Well, we must be going," said Mrs. Bradley uneasily. "Until a week from Sunday, Captain!" For the first time she took notice of David. "Bye-bye, little man!" She smirked, and David knew instantly that she was ill at ease with children.

As the van and the jeep drew away from each other, David felt he could burst with questions. "Who are they? Do you think she really has six cats? What did—?"

"Not now, David. I don't want to talk about them just now. It would take the edge off my homecoming, and coming home is always a special moment for me." Then he gave David a severe glance. "Just one thing. You stay clear of Carlos Jones."

"That's a funny name. I mean the combination—Carlos and Jones."

"Not in the canyon. There's a Pedro O'Reilly, and Lincoln Martinez is a close neighbor."

"And he's funny looking," David persisted.

"As funny as a rattlesnake in your closet. I've had trouble with him. He used to organize commercial dog fights. He had a ring in an old corral at Lago Seco."

"Dogs fighting in a ring? Wow! That must be exciting! Championship kind of fights? I'll bet Blaze would be a champ!"

"Would you like that?" Cappy asked quietly. "Would you like to see Blaze covered with some weaker dog's blood? Would you want him to commit murder when it's not natural to him? Oh, yes, Blaze could kill most other dogs, but soon those beautiful ears of his would be torn off, and he'd be lamed—you'd never again see him run or jump or play."

"Cappy, you don't mean the dogs fight to death!" David shuddered.

"Death or the next thing to it. And they only do it because some evil man like Carlos Jones has trained them by torture and brutality. All for the sake of winning a few bets and selling some tickets to a bloodbath!" There was quiet rage in Cappy's voice. "Dogs are more peaceful than people. Most of them go through their whole lives without one serious fight. Oh, there's snapping and threatening and sometimes a really hard bite or two. But usually it's not serious."

"But dogs *do* fight," David insisted.

"Sure. They defend their territory against intruders— and the dog that's stepped over the line usually runs away even if he's stronger. They'll fight over mating and sometimes because of other jealousies. But except for a crazy one now and then, they don't fight over nothing and they usually don't fight very hard. The man who first said dog-eat-dog didn't know much about animals."

A moment later Cappy stopped the van, letting the motor idle. They were at the top of a little rise, a low hill where the stream had cut a waterfall whose mists made a rainbow in the sunshine. Farther down the road a stone bridge spanned the white water and four willow trees marked the entrance to a driveway winding toward an adobe house with a rambling log porch and a stone chimney where vines wove their way to the roof tiles. Near the house stood another low building constructed of old faded bricks whose maroon shades were aging to violets and browns. On two sides of it, shaded by ash trees and softened by shrubbery, chain-link fences outlined kennel runs that were now deserted.

David sighed and smiled to see a tall whirring windmill rising above a brick spring house, and there were sunflowers just as his father had said there were, and a big tree that once had held a tree house. Near it split rails formed a circle that David took to be a corral, and far past the corral on a slope two tiny girls in straw hats and calico dresses were tending a flock of sheep, both animals and children dwarfed by the rock cliffs of Spirit Canyon that towered beyond a distant stretch of trees.

He knew all about it, it was just as he had imagined the scene, only better. And he turned his face toward the window so Cappy could not see the stupid tears gathering in his eyes, tears that were unreasonable because this was not a sad moment but a completely happy one.

"Rancho San Pascual," said Cappy, not really speaking to David. "I like stopping just here for a moment when I've been away for a while. This is the prettiest place in the world."

They drove over a cattle guard at the bridge, and the clanking of its pipes seemed to be a signal that started a loud and dismal howling audible all the way from the house.

"I didn't think there were any dogs here," said David.

"There aren't," Cappy answered without thinking, then chuckled. "I don't count old Xenia. She's the house dog, the one who's always slept at the foot of my bed—or on my bed. She's the special one with the run of the house—always has been ever since she was a pup."

"She must be beautiful."

"No, nothing special. Coat's thin, hindquarters were always too high. Ears aren't the best, either."

"Did she win a lot of prizes for other things?"

"Prizes? Xenia? Oh, Lord, no. Too stubborn."

"Well, then why's she so special?"

Cappy considered this as they drove to the house. "Well, Xenia knew from the day her eyes opened that she loved me most, that she was my dog. She told me so, and once I realized that, it didn't much matter that she wasn't very pretty and couldn't do much." Cappy frowned and a note of exasperation came into his voice. "Lord, boy, I can't answer such a question! There aren't any reasons in this life—no use looking for them."

Blaze, hearing Xenia, began his own baying, increasing his volume to match old Xenia's as she hobbled from the house. It was deafening, ear splitting. And it sounded like home to Cappy.

Mrs. Littlefoot, a widow for as long as anyone could remember, had come to Rancho San Pascual a quarter of a century ago as a laundress, then stayed to nurse Cappy's dying wife, and had reigned as cook and housekeeper ever since. Her black hair, now flecked with gray, hung in two thick braids that dangled halfway to her waist and were tied with little bows to match the flower print dresses she always wore on weekdays.

She worked bareheaded in the other rooms of the house, but in the kitchen she always put on a straw hat and tucked her braids under it. Years ago one of the braids had caught fire at the kerosene stove, and Mrs. Littlefoot was not a woman to stumble twice on the same stone. Besides, the white scar on her brown cheek was always there to remind her of danger.

Since one of her ancestors had been Spanish and she herself was a Catholic, Mrs. Littlefoot considered herself a "native," along with the majority of people who lived in Spirit Canyon and in the three villages near it. The other inhabitants were either Indians, like many of her cousins, or Anglos, like Cappy.

Mrs. Littlefoot betrayed neither surprise nor pleasure at David's arrival, yet he felt that in her silent way she welcomed him, even though she only said, "You have your father's eyebrows and ears, so I know what to watch out for." Then she pinched the flesh of his upper arm so suddenly that he jumped. "Skinny! Like your father, God remember him. You will drink a big glass of goat's milk every day. Your father used to try to pour the milk out the window, but I saw him with the eyes in the back of my head."

David knew that people couldn't have eyes in the back of their heads, but it was almost possible to believe Mrs.

Littlefoot was an exception. He studied her covertly, finding her strong cheekbones and sharp chin very fierce, yet he liked the warmth of her voice, and when she forgot her fierceness and smiled, she was transformed.

She led David to a long narrow room with a tile floor and a tile roof supported by aspen beams whose crookedness fascinated him since he had never imagined anyone building anything with wood that was not straight. An Indian blanket with a soaring thunderbird hung on the wall above the rope and tick bed. Tall windows had sills just above the floor, and looking out David saw Cappy standing near the chain-link fence of a kennel run talking to Blaze, who sat quietly in his new home.

"Bolt the shutters at night," Mrs. Littlefoot cautioned him. "Who knows what comes on the night air?"

David examined several framed photographs standing on the mantle of the stone fireplace. He knew that the boy in the pictures must be his father, but since he could not remember his father looking at all like this, the photos were not sad, only curious. In one of them the boy pointed to a huge, catlike animal that hung dead from the limb of a tree.

"A mountain lion?" David asked, eyes wide.

Mrs. Littlefoot nodded. "A puma. He used to kill sheep. The dogs tracked him and your grandfather shot him."

"Here at San Pascual?"

"No, no. Far up the canyon near the Three Caves."

David asked, "Three Caves? What are they?"

"Who knows? People talk about them, but I have never seen them. Maybe there are no such caves." She turned away, gesturing toward a wardrobe cabinet. "Hang your clothes there. Now I must cook supper. If you need anything, I will be in the kitchen." Then she hesitated, put her hand on his shoulder, studied him, nodded approval, and left.

After she had gone, David examined the other photographs, finding one that did not show the boy. This was a colored picture of a dog that looked like Blaze—then, a second later, he saw that it was not like Blaze at all, and understood for the first time that all good German Shepherd Dogs looked something alike, yet were all very different. The dog in the picture was not so dark as Blaze and had more burnt gold. His eyes were lighter and not quite so wise looking. David quickly decided that Blaze had better, bigger ears and was altogether more beautiful. The dog lay on a rainbow-striped rug, resting yet alert as he looked inquiringly at the camera.

Glancing toward the floor beside his new bed, David recognized the rainbow rug, its colors pallid now. His father's dog had slept there—his father's dog, his father's bed. For a second the white mountain returned to him, its snow dazzling, then it faded when he heard his grandfather calling him.

"Yes, Cappy! Coming!" he answered, stepping through the unscreened window.

Cappy stood at the door of the brick building that housed the kennels. "I want you to feed Blaze, then we'll take a walk with him before supper."

"Can I, Cappy? Will he let me?"

"Yes, I think so. I'll be with you, and something else

has changed. In the van Blaze was on his own ground where he felt protective. Here, he's a stranger and dogs are cautious in unfamiliar places. That's why a dog wandering alone on a street or a lost dog usually isn't dangerous unless it's frightened or hurt."

The kitchen in the kennel building gleamed with stainless steel and enamel. David inspected scales and measuring containers, dustproof cabinets and bins. The room was like a scientist's laboratory, nothing at all like the kitchen for humans in the house where everything was casual, a little run down.

"You measure out the food mixture like this, David. Add some ground meat. Here the meat's usually ground scraps of mutton because this is sheep country."

Cappy mixed the food, then turned it out in a metal pan. "Never, never use a plastic dish for food or water for a German Shepherd. Remember that!"

"Why not, Cappy? On television—"

"What you *don't* see on television are dogs being cut open by a veterinary surgeon because they've chewed up a plastic dish. Dogs can't digest plastic and sharp pieces are like broken glass inside them. No plastic toys, either, and no plastic bottles left lying around. Plain poison!

"We'll feed him in the yard since we've got only one dog," said Cappy, ending his sermon on plastic.

"What about Xenia?"

"Xenia eats in the kitchen near the stove. She wouldn't touch a bite anywhere else. She has Mrs. Littlefoot and me well trained."

Cappy left the dish of food behind, just inside the kennel door, then opened a low gate to release Blaze from the fenced run. The dog bounded and barked, a whoop of delight at being reunited with Cappy; he jumped, trying to put his paws on Cappy's shoulders, and seemed not the least offended when Cappy clipped him sharply with a raised fist, knocking him aside. "Down, Blaze! Down!"

But Blaze eyed David with suspicion and would not approach him. "Sit on the ground," said Cappy, and David sat. The old man sauntered over to David and joined him, also sitting on the ground. "Talk to him, David." David began talking, but at the sound of his voice, Blaze barked. David's heart sank.

"That bark isn't a warning," Cappy said. "Listen to it! That's a confusion bark. Blaze doesn't know what he's supposed to do, how to behave. So he's barking to hide his confusion."

Suddenly Blaze raced in a wide circle, still barking, although his tone had changed. Still going full speed, he leaped into the air, then rolled over on the ground twice, paws wildly kicking the air.

"An actor!" exclaimed Cappy. "He's showing off for us. I think we're watching the discovery of a new talent."

His performance over, Blaze came confidently to Cappy, his tail wagging, proud of his new accomplishment as an entertainer. He ignored David.

"Good boy! Good fellow!" Cappy praised him, then said to David. "Touch him now. Scratch him under the chest bones. Be firm and not the least shy."

David put out his hand, not quite able to disguise his timidity. Blaze was so big, so very big standing over him as he sat on the ground. He remembered the bared teeth in the van—the thought of the snarling still frightened him.

But then his hand was actually in the dog's fur as though he had plunged it into a great mat of fine silk. Blaze, gazing into Cappy's face, paid no attention yet seemed contented, so David scratched a little harder, digging in his fingers, feeling under the thick hair and smooth skin a heavy breastbone, and it was like touching rock. Then the dog slowly turned his great head and looked down at him, studying him with a judicious gaze. The black nose twitched once.

"Blaze, Blaze," David whispered. The dog's eyes seemed deep and knowing. After a moment he put his head on David's shoulder, and David felt the broad, moist tongue lightly touching his ear, kissing him.

"I think this is the start of a friendship," said Cappy. "Now give him his dinner, but move slowly. Don't surprise him in any way."

As David went to get the food dish, Cappy called to him, "Put the dish on the ground fast. He hasn't got any table manners yet, and if you keep moving that slowly, he might knock you down by accident when he rushes the food."

As Cappy suspected, David had a narrow escape when Blaze smelled food and dashed to get it. They stood together, watching Blaze, Cappy frowning and shaking his head in disapproval. "He goes for food like a pig. Not from hunger, either, it's plain lack of confidence in the next meal. Lord, he needs civilizing!"

David nodded. "When do we begin, Cappy?"

Cappy, who had been in a reverie, looked surprised. "Begin what?"

"Civilizing him." David did not dare look at Cappy, and the next few seconds seemed the longest of his life.

Cappy studied Blaze. The dog had finished eating and now stood alert, watching his human companions. Blaze leaned slightly forward, his hindquarters low and poised, the full feathered tail just brushing the grass. His coat and ruff glowed jet and tawny in the thickening light, his eyes, now shadowed, were no longer dark gold but two bright points of obsidian. Even standing absolutely still, Cappy thought, Blaze conveyed a sense of motion and power the way a drawn bow conveys a sense of the arrow's speed.

Of the German Shepherd Dogs he had bred—every breeding done with so much care and hope—Blaze now struck him as the most beautiful he had produced in a life-time, the nearest to perfection. Blaze was the culmination but he had come too late and his mind had been twisted and harmed.

He looked from the dog to the waiting boy. These two were the final products of his life—a boy he did not un-derstand and a dog he distrusted.

Blaze walked slowly to David's side and sat waiting.

"I think we should start tomorrow morning," Cappy said at last.

Mrs. Littlefoot served them supper at the big round table in the kitchen, filling their plates with a pungent stew. She herself did not sit down, but ate standing at the drainboard, her long braids firmly tucked under her hat.

"What's the news of the canyon?" Cappy asked.

She considered the question. "The ghost dog came again two nights ago."

Cappy raised an eyebrow. "Where?"

"On that rock at the top of Little Hump. I heard it wailing."

"Howling?"

"No, wailing. I looked out and saw it in the moonlight."

"A ghost dog?" David asked eagerly. "What color?"

"Ghost color." Mrs. Littlefoot turned to the stove to take hot tortillas from the warming oven. "Gray and white and silver. The moon shines through it and it casts no shadow."

"A coyote," said Cappy.

"No. Xenia heard it too. She hid in that little space behind the bathtub where she thinks nothing can find her."

Xenia, lying in a corner, thumped her tail proudly, hearing her name and confident of praise. She was waiting impatiently for the aroma of coffee being poured, which was a signal that the meal was over and she could approach and lie at Cappy's feet.

"Maybe a stray from the village," said Cappy, knowing he could not convince Mrs. Littlefoot. Her world was filled with goblins: a flying head that rode storm winds, a dwarf whose specialty was carrying off women doing laundry at the river, and despite going faithfully to Mass, she believed firmly in three Indian gods, one a giant serpent, another an eagle, and the third a puma. These voracious gods lived in caves far back in the mountains but were quite capable of descending at any time.

"What besides the ghost dog?" Cappy asked.

"Carlos Jones is back and has gone to work for the Woman."

Since Mrs. Bradley was this year's topic of gossip there was no need to name her.

"I know. I passed them on the road."

"He is living in a cabin on her land. It is dangerous to have such a man for a neighbor," she said. "He will end worse than his father who was shot while stealing rabbits from a pen. Not stealing horses or even sheep, but rabbits!" Then she said something to Cappy in Spanish.

"Don't worry," he answered. "I'll watch out. There's nothing Jones can do."

"City people should stay in the cities. Something unlucky will happen to the Woman. Everyone knows it."

When Mrs. Littlefoot poured coffee, Xenia came confidently to the table, and Cappy automatically scratched behind her ears. She rubbed her head against his knee, blissful, and David imagined Blaze sitting beside his own chair, magnificent and devoted. But Cappy had already explained that Blaze must never be allowed in a room with Xenia, because she would be jealous and would probably attack Blaze, who was far too strong and rough for her.

After supper Cappy went through his small accumulation of mail, tossing Mrs. Bradley's coy cocktail invitation in the wastebasket. "Silly woman!"

David watched Mrs. Littlefoot cook liver Cappy had ordered so he could reward Blaze tomorrow when the dog did well in training. When Cappy had told her he wanted the liver, she nodded and her expression did not change, but now David noticed that she was smiling slightly and her eyes had a faraway look as she stirred the bits of meat that were slowly drying and hardening in the frying pan. He wondered what she was thinking—he knew it had to do with the liver—and it puzzled him that her usually unexpressive face should now show pleasure and sadness at the same time. It was, he decided, very complicated.

At nine o'clock Cappy tried to telephone the apartment in San Francisco, but again there was no answer, and at nine-thirty David went to bed in the long narrow room that now smelled even more strongly of cedar wood, and aspen, and split piñon logs that were in a basket near the hearth.

But he did not fall asleep. After putting out the lamp, he took a small flashlight from his camping kit and in its beam examined the photographs he took from the mantle. The great brown puma his grandfather had shot at a place called the Three Caves caught his imagination, and he pictured himself strolling along a mountain trail, a rifle cradled in his arms and Blaze padding happily at his side. Then Blaze seemed to freeze, gave a growl of warning, and in the nick of time David saw the huge cat crouched in ambush on a rock ledge, its yellow eyes burning with hate and ferocity. It lunged and David fired, catching it in midair, and the beast fell dead at his feet, its unsheathed claws just scratching the toe of his boot. Blaze had saved him and he had saved Blaze.

He stretched in his bed, tired yet not ready for sleep, and

for a long time he stared into the darkness, his mind returning to the picture of the rainbow rug with the dog lying on it, the rug he could touch if he reached over the edge of the mattress.

Then, suddenly and very clearly, he knew what to do. Slipping from the bed, he went to the window and opened the shutters Mrs. Littlefoot had fastened against the night. A cool wind had flooded down from the peaks of the sierra, and it billowed the thin curtains, riffling his hair, bringing the presence of the mountain into the room, a freshness of pine, and its cold touch made him sense the white peaks with snows that never melted.

He stepped over the low sill and moved into the moonlight and shadows. A whippoorwill, perched in the dark tangle of the ash tree, challenged him with an eerie, lonely question in an almost human voice. Then the bird fell silent and a tiny furry animal skittered across the pale yard, making for cover in the blackness of the meadowsweet bush as a shadow swept by, the spread wings of a horned owl moving in great silent circles, scanning the corners of the night.

Stiff grass pricked the bare soles of his feet as he ran across the yard toward the kennels. And there Blaze was waiting for him, sitting tall eared and expectant, quietly alert at the gait of his run. David slipped back the unlocked bolt while Blaze, unmoving, watched him.

"Come, Blaze! Come with me!"

Then they were running together in the night, around the dim circle of the empty corral, past the windmill and the shuttered well house. They ran as David had only imagined they could run, his own body light as air, his legs strong and well mended. Blaze leaped high into the moonlight, and David laughed aloud, clapping his hands together, thinking of a dolphin bursting from dark water to crash into the sunshine, glittering, as Blaze's silver undercoat glittered now. Throwing his arms above his head, flapping them like wings, David bounded with Blaze across the meadow, flying.

He flew to his own window, Blaze landing with him, and together they entered the room. While David put on the lamp and closed the shutters, Blaze inspected the corners, peered under the bed, checked the wardrobe, confident but questioning.

When David sat on the faded rainbow rug, Blaze, after turning around twice, lay down beside him, and a moment later remained there quietly after David turned out the light and slipped between the covers of his bed and rested his head on the white pillow. He fell asleep and dreamed of flying, of a great lift of mountain wind carrying him and Blaze upward, launching them above the house, above the chimney, where they soared past the windmill to skim the walls of the canyon. David's hand dangled from the side of the mattress, came to rest on Blaze's back, and the dog stirred in sleep but did not awaken.

That was the way Cappy found them in the morning.

Five

The project for civilizing Blaze and changing him from
an outlaw into what Cappy called a "respectable, law-
abiding canine citizen" almost ended the same morning it
began when one near-disaster followed another.

At six-thirty Cappy, unaware of the change in Blaze's
sleeping place, opened the door of David's room. He
opened it silently and took one very quiet step inside,
wondering if David, after the long trip, should be allowed
to sleep later. He could not remember relevant details
from Ben's childhood, but he knew nothing exhausted a
puppy more than a change of environment, and he supposed little boys reacted the same way.

The room, its shutters bolted, was almost dark, but in
the dim light from the partly open door he saw David's
tousled head on the pillow and a memory stirred gently in
him. Then for an instant he thought his eyes were playing
him tricks or perhaps Mrs. Littlefoot's ghost dog had actually materialized. The ghost of a well-remembered dog
named Sinbad appeared to be sleeping where the living
Sinbad had slept for ten years.

Cappy did not quite gasp before realizing with some consternation that the dog was Blaze, that David had spirited him into the house, once again showing more determination and independence than good judgment. A lecture was necessary, Cappy decided, a stern talk about playing with fire, and he would deliver it even though the boy and the dog seemed happy together and Cappy had never believed in wasting time worrying about what might have happened but hadn't.

They must have had quite a night, Cappy thought. A night of racing around the meadow to judge from how heavily both the boy and the dog now slept. Well, this would be David's last nocturnal adventure at San Pascual.

Yet Cappy hesitated, looking at this new version of a once familiar scene, surprised at the emotions the picture evoked in him. Then, chiding himself for turning sentimental, he decided to let the boy sleep a little longer, and started to turn away.

When he touched the door, a hinge creaked and the high-pitched sound came faintly to Blaze's ears, causing him to stir and half open his eyes. A door that had not been open last night was strangely open now, and silhouetted against the light Blaze saw a menacing figure, a man who lurked in the room and must have entered with furtive quiet. Blaze, not fully awake, did not recognize the intruder and instant signals of danger flashed from his brain—a menace, an enemy to be driven off. Even as a growl was forming in his throat, Blaze charged to attack.

Cappy had sensed what was about to happen even before he heard the growl. Snatching up a wooden chair that stood beside the door, he blocked the assault before Blaze was fully in action, but even so the dog's power knocked him backward hard against the wall.

"Blaze!" he yelled. "Blaze!" The dog, pulling back for a new assault, instantly recognized the voice. He blinked, tilting his head a little to see more clearly in the dim room, then the bristling fur smoothed, and without even looking sheepish or ashamed, Blaze trotted forward happily, eager to wish his friend good morning and unaware that he might have caused alarm or given offense.

Cappy still gripped the back of the chair with both hands as David sat up in bed, eyes wide, mouth agape.

Cappy, after opening the shutters, glowered at both the boy and the dog. "Well, it's nice to start the day with a little surprise! I suppose tonight you'll bring a puma in."

"What happened?" David asked, suddenly awake and very frightened.

"I came in unexpectedly and Blaze jumped me," said Cappy. "He was still asleep. Most guard dogs sleep half alert, but this one's like the tautest wire in a piano."

"I'm sure Blaze didn't mean any harm." The boy hesitated, looked at Cappy uncertainly before he spoke. "I suppose if you'd knocked on the door, he'd have expected you."

"*Expected me!*" Cappy's mouth opened, he turned red, then smothered the explosion he'd meant to let loose. No, he had not thought of knocking, and in the last years he had forgotten he should not walk into another person's room unannounced, even if that person was a small boy and his own grandson.

"Then next time I'll knock," he said gruffly. "But you'll make no other changes in arrangements around here without consulting me. Do you have that straight, young fellow?"

"Yes, sir," said David reasonably.

After breakfast they went to the corral, which Cappy called "the training ring." Blaze frisked beside them, ran off to pursue a butterfly, carefree and well meaning as a puppy.

"Don't hope for much," Cappy warned David. "It's hard to salvage a dog—or a child—who's been abused too long. Blaze is angry, David. This morning we found out he's even angry when he's asleep. He expects to be hurt, so he's afraid."

"Afraid? I don't think Blaze is afraid of anything."

"I don't mean he's cowardly. This is a different kind of fear, a sort of hitting back in advance. It's the fear that causes most of the dog bites that happen anywhere. So be prepared for disappointment, David. Maybe Blaze has been too badly hurt ever to be trusted."

"He's beautiful," said David.

"Yes," Cappy agreed, sighing.

But at first everything went so well that Cappy wondered if he had misjudged Blaze. The dog sat smartly at Cappy's left while a slip-chain collar was put over his head, seeming almost at military attention except for his wagging tail. Cappy left the collar on for only a few minutes, then removed it and showed David how it worked. "The steel links are light but strong. The slip collar gives you control—once you understand how to use it. Remember, for strong control, keep it up just behind Blaze's ears."

"I thought training collars had spikes or points on the inside to make the dog mind," said David.

"Not at San Pascual! Suppose you'd been trained with torture equipment. How would you feel about the world? Ready to chew it up, I'll bet."

Something was troubling David, and at last he spoke. "I don't understand how these things you talk about will make Blaze any more civilized. What does learning to heel or to jump have to do with not being crazy?"

"It's all part of an idea called *control*, David. Usually a dog who understands and obeys about a dozen commands somehow learns other things at the same time. He becomes a happier, more stable dog." Cappy knew that this was not the full answer. Good training often changed a dog's character, but he could not explain why. "Maybe it's like soldiers learning to march in formation. There's more to it than just moving a crowd from one place to another. Soldiers absorb attitudes and ideas at the same time, I'm told. Anyway, that's the best I can do to explain it."

Cappy had David put the collar on Blaze. "Now the leash. It's flat leather and just as long as I'm tall. Too long for you, but don't ever twist it around your arm."

He showed David how to hold the leash while Blaze romped and frisked with energy that never seemed to flag.

"Blaze seemed to know a leash, so we won't worry about its being unfamiliar to him. But remember, he weighs more than you do, and he's got four feet to give him power and balance. You can't handle him by pulling the leash, so you *jerk* it, don't pull it. Say that over and over to yourself."

"Jerk, don't pull," said David several times.

"When he does well, praise him. When he goes wrong, you make a big fuss and yell 'Phooey!' as loud as you can."

"Phooey?" David asked. "Why?"

"It's a noisy word, it starts off with a little explosion. Oh, lots of words might work, but phooey's a good one."

When David called, Blaze trotted to his side, a model of canine deportment, and sat quietly while David fastened the harness snap of the leash on the proper collar ring.

"Just take an easy little walk," said Cappy. "We won't worry about heeling yet."

They began walking, David taking a few steps forward, starting on the left foot, the foot next to Blaze, as Cappy had told him. They walked around the ring easily and David, confident of Blaze and finding the leash too long, let it twist around his arm.

"David, don't let the leash—"

Blaze moved ahead, enough that the collar tightened sharply, and at that instant, as Cappy later said, "All hell broke loose."

Blaze felt the restricting pull of the line, and a hateful memory surged in him—the strangling chain that slid along the wire in George Blout's yard. He knew again his desperate struggles when water and shade were just beyond reach, and now as the thing around his throat tightened, he rebelled and fought it, hurling himself wildly ahead, pitting his strength against whatever held him. At the same time, he turned his head to slash at the leash, struggling to bite through this maddening, confining strap.

Blaze's first lunge threw David to the ground, and unable to let go of the twisted leash, he found himself dragged across the ring face down.

Cappy never knew how he managed to cover the distance between them in what seemed like one leap. Throwing himself on top of David, he then rolled forward to pin the leash to the ground with the weight of his body. For a few seconds the dog strained and struggled, then with a faint snap the steel slip chain broke, freeing Blaze, who went dashing in frantic circles around the ring.

Cappy managed to get to his knees—he did not yet trust himself to stand. "Are you all right, boy?"

"Uh huh," murmured David, gingerly touching his arm where the leather had burned his skin. Scratches smarted on his cheek and forehead, and when he touched his chin, he brushed away fine gravel. For a moment he struggled to catch his breath—he thought he would never stop panting—then said, "Where can I find another collar, Cappy?"

Cappy shook his head, still breathless. They should get rid of this crazy dog, he thought. Get rid of him before the dog accidentally injured one of them or intentionally injured someone else.

David, looking at Cappy's face, read his thoughts, and his eyes dropped to the ground, he spoke awkwardly. "I think a bee stung him, Cappy. I'm almost sure of it. I saw some bees a little while ago—or maybe they were hornets."

Cappy shook his head. "No. More likely they were Furies."

"What do you mean?"

"If he was stung, David, it was by something from his past, something that stings harder than any hornet. But never mind. Let's go to the house and wash, get some of this grit out of my hair, and we'd better disinfect these scratches. Mrs. Littlefoot can mend that shirt of yours like new."

When Cappy stood up, he realized that this evening every joint in his body would ache. Something in his left shoulder seemed pulled loose and both his kneecaps were skinned. He was too old for this, too old to be fighting and throwing himself on the ground. He should never have started this hopeless work—it was a fool's mistake.

Blaze approached, his world right again, and nuzzled Cappy's hand, then lay down, rolled over, and kicked his paws in the air playfully.

"You must have come across the ring in one leap, Cappy."

"Well, they say a grasshopper can jump eighty times his own length. Guess I'm part grasshopper."

David looked up at him. "Anyway, you move fast, faster than anybody. Maybe someday I can do that, too."

Cappy smiled at him, then nodded gravely. "Yes, David. Someday you will. All it takes is a little practice— and I've had a lot of that."

That afternoon Cappy, despite stiffening joints, decided to try again with Blaze, to work for an hour, although he had little hope that the dog would respond. David could watch, but Cappy would handle Blaze himself, taking no second chance that David might be hurt.

But after a few minutes of walking Blaze around the corral, Cappy forgot that his back muscles had seemed tied in knots. Blaze, now calm and assured, showed not the least skittishness, even in accepting the leash after being allowed to inspect it carefully and drag it after him.

"That's what I should have done this morning," said Cappy. "You let a puppy discover the leash for himself. But I didn't think of Blaze as a puppy—my mistake!"

Blaze sat with his head cocked, ears alert and eyes sparkling as he concentrated on every word Cappy spoke, listened for every changing intonation, trying to understand. Until the past few days no human had ever spoken to him except to shout, so now it seemed strange yet soothing and reassuring to hear quiet voices speaking to him and around him.

But even more important than his discovery of language was his discovery of love. When he had first met Cappy he had felt a tugging of emotion, and a little later a not quite sure sense of belonging. Yesterday this new feeling had expanded to include David, and then last night, after running with David in the meadow, he had gone to sleep contented, knowing he had at last come home.

Cappy, too, felt an unfamiliar contentment as he worked with Blaze while David, sitting on a rail of the corral, watched admiringly. He felt refreshed and vaguely realized that despite his aches, this was the first time in months that he had not the faintest sense of being a little tired, a little run down. He was doing what he had always loved most, working with an eager, intelligent dog on a fine, clear day. And because of this love there was nothing in life he could do so well. Also it had become important that David understand what he was doing and what it meant, although Cappy could not explain why this understanding suddenly seemed necessary.

The allotted hour went by, became an hour and a half, then almost two hours before Cappy looked at his watch. "That's enough. In fact, it's far too much. You never let training become hard work. It's got to be a game—a serious one, but still a game. We don't want to tire him."

"He doesn't seem tired," said David, watching Blaze caper in half-serious pursuit of a grasshopper.

"Well, if he's not, I am." Yet there was a new lightness in Cappy's step as they went to the spring house where David pumped cool water for all three of them.

At supper that evening they talked over every detail of what had happened during the day, laughing at the memory of rolling on the ground, forgetting how much it had hurt at the time. Mrs. Littlefoot watched them without saying a word, standing at the drainboard holding her plate, chewing her food slowly and thoughtfully.

After the table had been cleared and Xenia had received her proper attention, Cappy brought out an old manual that had stood unopened on a shelf for years, and showed David drawings of various hand signals used in dog training.

"Blaze learns three times as much by eye as he does by ear, so always use the gesture with the word. Eventually you won't need words at all. That would be handy if you were in a situation where you couldn't make noise, when you had to command silently. Long ago I trained war dogs that way."

As David looked at the manual, he imagined himself peering through the tangled foliage of a jungle where bandits lurked everywhere. He made a small, soundless gesture, and Blaze, across a clearing, dropped to earth, hiding behind bushes, concealed but still keeping his eyes fixed on David, awaiting the next silent, strategic command.

Cappy and David went through the entire book, practicing every gesture, while Xenia, half asleep, watched them, now and then thumping her tail to show she approved and even understood a few commands, although she had no intention of obeying any of them. At bedtime David, with permission tonight, went to the kennel run to bring Blaze in to sleep on the faded rug by the bed.

That night Cappy forgot to try calling San Francisco, and Mrs. Littlefoot, although she noticed this, did not remind him.

For David the next few days were magical as he learned about this new world he had entered, a small universe bounded on one side by the swift, shallow stream and on the other three by rambling wire fences that marked out the extent of Rancho San Pascual. David and Blaze could walk these limits in half an hour.

The dog and the boy were always together, for contrary to what Cappy had feared, once Blaze had given his devotion, he was constant and steady. David had no other companion except a few imaginary friends and several foes he had invented, yet he was never lonely. Blaze's company was enough, and Blaze in turn never strayed far from David.

During those days David's world had only three inhabitants besides himself—Cappy, Blaze, and Mrs. Littlefoot. Xenia did not count, for she had retired into her private sphere and was interested only in watching and sometimes stiffly following Cappy. She tolerated Mrs. Littlefoot and ignored David.

On the edge of this world a few other creatures loitered or passed. Every day David saw at a distance the flock of grayish sheep tended by the two small Indian girls, but they never came close to the San Pascual boundaries.

Twice he saw Mrs. Bradley's flower-bedecked jeep on the road, but too far away for him to know if the hawk-faced man, Carlos Jones, was driving. David could remember nothing of Jones's face except its sharpness, but he had a clear and dreadful recollection of the man's long-fingered hand resting on the door of the jeep. Mrs. Littlefoot had told him about a pair of chopped-off hands that crawled the canyon at night pinching and slapping naughty children who ventured out after dark. Her grim tone made him suspect that the bodiless hands did much worse things than slapping, and since he felt sure the hands resembled those of Carlos Jones, the sight of the jeep sent a delicious chill of fear through him.

One morning a dark, silent little boy was found standing at the far side of the bridge holding a black and white spotted puppy in his arms. He had been too shy or too polite to approach the house or to shout to make his presence known, so he might have stood there for hours had not Mrs. Littlefoot happened to step outside to shake a tablecloth.

He spoke neither English nor Spanish but Mrs. Littlefoot understood his whispered words, although she would have known anyway that he had come because the puppy seemed near death and Cappy had become famous in the canyon as a healer of animals. Not wanting to risk bringing infection near Blaze or Xenia, Mrs. Littlefoot summoned Cappy to the bridge and David followed, leaving Blaze locked in the kennel run.

The boy was no bigger than David but there was something ancient and solemn about him as he held out the puppy for Cappy to examine. It was a sad little creature, skin and sharp bones with rheumy eyes and a distended belly. The puppy's whine sounded like a hopeless plea as it summoned its strength to lick Cappy's fingers.

"Go to the kennel kitchen," Cappy told David. "In the cupboard to the right of the sink you'll find a metal box like a tackle box. Bring it here."

David had no trouble finding the right cupboard. All the cabinets, drawers, bins, and canisters were labeled in Cappy's precise printing. Most of the labels were ordinary, such as "Food Supplements," "Grooming Aids," and "Shipping Forms." But one drawer was mysteriously marked "Thingamajigs" and next to it was "Whatchacallits." On a lower shelf stood a box for "Unidentified Objects for Unimaginable Uses." David resolved to investigate when he had more time.

Opening the cupboard marked "Medical," he found the tackle box, then paused, standing on tiptoe, to inspect the higher shelf of the cupboard. Why, he wondered, would Cappy have an impressive microscope protected by a transparent plastic cover? Beside it stood a whole rack of empty test tubes such as he'd seen in television programs about scientists.

David hurried back to the bridge where Cappy opened the box and searched among the bottles, tubes, and jars. He filled a small rubber syringe, and squirted a liquid down the puppy's throat, causing it to gag and vomit up foamy fluids.

"Roundworms!" exclaimed Cappy. "The poor baby is riddled with them. Well, thank the Lord it's something I can handle. The pup's really too weak for worming, but there isn't any choice."

Cappy motioned for the boy to watch, put a brown pill on the back of the puppy's tongue, then, holding its jaws shut, gently massaged the animal's throat until the pill was swallowed.

Cappy wrapped two more pills in a twist of paper, gave them to the boy, speaking slowly while Mrs. Littlefoot translated. "Give the puppy a second pill tomorrow when the sun stands where it is now. The next morning, take an aspen stick and cut a notch in it. Do this every morning and when the stick has as many notches as you have fingers, give your dog the second pill and God will make her well, I think."

The boy nodded, reached into the pocket of his ragged jeans and brought out several coins, holding out his palm so Cappy could pick out his proper fee.

"Thank you." Cappy nodded gravely and selected a nickel and two greasy pennies. The boy lifted his small brown hand in a gesture of salute, then trudged away, clasping the puppy to his chest.

"Are you a doctor for animals, Cappy?" David asked.

"A veterinarian? No. But there's no veterinarian anywhere near here—you have to go all the way to the city. Not many people can do that, so I help if the trouble's something I understand and if I'm sure the animal's owner can't get to a real veterinarian."

"I saw a microscope in the cupboard. What do you use it for?"

"I don't use it. It belonged to your father when he was a student. He was studying to become our veterinarian here, but then he met your mother and changed his mind." Cappy turned away and knelt to snap the buckles of the tackle box shut. "I suppose the whole idea of that career was more my wish than his anyhow." Cappy shook his head, sighing, then shrugged and stood up quickly. "Now take this box back where you found it."

"May I look through the microscope, Cappy?"

"No, not yet." He hesitated, then put his hand lightly on David's shoulder. "But in a few years, if you're still interested in it, I'll give it to you for your own."

That afternoon David went down to the river intending to catch a trout, a doomed ambition because Blaze quickly discovered the joy of leaping into the shallow water and splashing it with his head, scaring off any fish. At sunset, when they went back to the house, Cappy was sitting on the back steps, looking thoughtfully at the changing sky, the slowly deepening purples and vermilions behind the far peaks. He was shortening a training leash, making it the right length for David to handle, and it now lay across his lap. David sat beside him and after a silence Cappy said, "Your uncle telephoned about an hour ago."

David's heart seemed to lurch. "From San Francisco?"

"No. From a hotel at Lake Tahoe. He'd called that camp where you're supposed to be. They told him to try here."

David reached down and touched Blaze, who was lying at his feet. He asked cautiously, "How is Uncle Arthur?"

"Mad enough to spit nails! For a minute I thought he was going to catch the next plane, come here, and drag you to California by the scruff of your neck, young man. But I persuaded him not to make any violent moves."

Arthur Wheeler's anger had surprised Cappy, who had always regarded him as affable but shallow, a harmlessly vain man with a salesman's show of confidence. But David's defection had struck Arthur as a personal attack and, Cappy suspected, even as an accusation of failure. Cappy had listened to a ten-minute tirade about Arthur's rights and injuries. *"The kid's got to learn, and I'll see to it, Cappy. He can't defy his Aunt Nadine and me and get away with it."*

"What did Uncle Arthur want?"

"That's a fool question!" Cappy spluttered, but sounded more upset than angry. "He wanted to know if you are, by some chance, still alive. Your uncle does have a certain interest in your health and whereabouts, although you're not exactly popular with him right now."

David avoided Cappy's glare, looking down as he petted Blaze. "Does he want me to go to that camp? To go back to San Francisco?"

"He doesn't care about the camp—except he's not overjoyed about the money wasted on camp fees. But of course he wants you to go back to San Francisco. What would make you think anything else?" Cappy hesitated, seemed suddenly interested in examining the mend in the leash. "But angry as your uncle sounded, I thought we'd better give him a while for his temper to cool. So I told him I needed you here this summer to help train Blaze. Naturally he and your aunt don't like having you away so long, and I'm not sure myself it's a good idea. Anyway, you can stay here until a week before school starts in the fall. That is, if you want to."

"I want to," said David, hardly breathing. Until fall? That was forever, a time in the unimaginable future that might never come. And he wanted to tell Cappy that he loved him, but he could not seem to make the words come right, and Cappy was suddenly acting strange and uneasy, avoiding his eyes.

"David, oh, David! I don't want you to be hurt, boy. You have to remember that this summer in the valley isn't forever, that growing up *means* going away. The summer's short and fall does come—always too soon, always before you know it or want it. And at the end of the summer, you go back to another life. Remember that, David!"

Cappy stood up abruptly. "Well, boy, we'd better put Blaze in his run and go clean up." His voice sounded gruff and rather jerky. "If we're not ready for supper, Mrs. Littlefoot'll skin us both alive."

All weekdays began the same way. After breakfast Cappy and David worked with Blaze for an hour, then rested for a few minutes in the coolness of the spring house. This routine done, David took Blaze on a tour of the San Pascual boundaries, a short hike he called "going on patrol," although he was not sure what he was looking for or guarding against. There were only a few rules and warnings for these expeditions: David and Blaze must stay within the limits of the ranch, keep an eye out for rattlesnakes, which were rare but not unknown in the lower part of Spirit Canyon, and David must never carry matches, let alone dream of lighting any kind of fire, since of all calamities a forest fire was the one most dreaded by Cappy and his neighbors.

The first three times David and Blaze made a morning patrol nothing of consequence happened except in David's imagination. Then on the fourth morning David began his patrol as usual at the bridge and walked east following the stream until they came to a wire-mesh fence camouflaged with vines Cappy had planted years ago. The fences at San Pascual were not high, only a little taller than David, and any grown German Shepherd dog could leap them easily, but none ever had since only the most reliable dogs had been given the freedom of the ranch when it was still a working kennel. The fences served as psychological barriers and kept out stray sheep and goats.

David and Blaze turned again when the fence angled sharply at the southeast corner of the ranch, the dog, unleashed, never venturing very far ahead or falling far behind. They crossed thinly forested land next, a long stretch where trees shaded the fence so heavily that in places the sun-starved vines had died, leaving the wire uncovered. On previous mornings David had noticed traces of a path just beyond the fence, thinking it might be one of the deer trails Cappy had talked about—at any rate it seemed little used since grass was beginning to blend it into the wooded meadow. David wondered if they might actually discover a herd of deer, and a vision of this replaced a daydream of desperados he had been enjoying. He was lost in this reverie when Blaze, moving a little ahead of him, suddenly halted, alert and on guard.

David tensed, took a cautious step forward, wondering if Blaze had sensed something exciting, but supposing it was only another rabbit or chipmunk. Then David realized that the unseen presence was nothing so harmless, for Blaze's fur began to bristle and he lifted his head, catching a scent, although he still gave no warning sound. Where they stood, the vines were so thin that David had a full view of the path beyond the fence, although it turned sharply just a few yards ahead, disappearing behind thick bushes.

Then the stranger, rounding this corner of the path, strode into view and Blaze uttered a loud, threatening growl. David gasped at the sight of the man. White trousers covered with reddish brown stains were tucked into muddy boots; he wore a broad leather belt decorated with porcupine quills, and instead of a shirt a vest made of the pelts of small animals crudely sewn together. But David only comprehended these details later. The astonishing thing was the dark bandanna tied around the man's face, masking him and making him look exactly like a stagecoach robber or one of the western bandits David had just been imagining. Above the bandanna and below a gray slouch hat two eyes as black and glittering as obsidian points were set beneath bushy brows.

For an instant the surprised man, the dog, and the boy seemed paralyzed, staring at one another silently, then Blaze and the stranger recovered their wits at the same time. Blaze barked furiously and the man, realizing that the low fence afforded no protection, leaped toward the nearest tree and began scrambling into its lower branches. David watched him, still dazed but realizing that the leather pouch strapped to the man's hip was not a gun holster after all but a sheath for a hunting knife. Alarmed and instinctively seeking protection, David put his hand on Blaze's shoulder, and it was only his touch that kept Blaze from jumping the fence to attack.

The man drew a curved long knife from the sheath, brandished it, and hooking his other arm around a branch, pointed three crooked fingers at David and Blaze, shouting words David could not understand but which sounded horrible, and as he waved his arm, David saw that there were bones and feathers and repulsive things that looked like the severed heads of birds tied to it with leather thongs. David suddenly imagined the knife being thrown with deadly aim.

"Come, Blaze!" David backed away several steps, then turned and started toward the house. "Come!"

The dog, after snarling a final threat, followed David, who forced himself to walk and not to run because some inner voice prompted him not to show panic. Behind, the man in the tree howled at them, a wailing cry of rage that made gooseflesh rise on David's arms.

When at last they reached the house, Cappy was not there, having gone to the village store, but Mrs. Littlefoot nodded as David described the man.

"No, he is not a desperado," she said. "He is a man who lives far up the canyon, and no one is permitted to see his face, so he always wears a scarf or a mask. I have heard that the masks are terrible—monsters and devilish animals."

"Why does he wear a mask? Is he so ugly?"

"Who knows if he is ugly or handsome? The mask is part of his magic. He is a witch, and for money he casts spells on people's enemies so they sicken or their sheep sicken and die. Sometimes their gardens wither. They say he plays wicked jokes like causing a pretty girl to grow a beard."

"Does he really have magic power?" David's eyes had widened.

"I am a Catholic," said Mrs. Littlefoot uneasily. "I do not believe such nonsense."

"What's his name?"

"It is unlucky to say his Indian name." Mrs. Littlefoot crossed herself. "The Anglos—like your grandfather—call him John the Baptist. That is probably unlucky, too."

"Why call him that?"

"Ask your grandfather. Now I have work to do, so go play with Blaze, or get the fish pole and try to catch a trout." She hesitated, then unexpectedly patted David on the head. "I have a better idea. Take this pan and the little ladder. Pick some cherries and I will make you a pie."

As he filled the pan, standing on top of the short ladder with Blaze lying nearby, David glanced from time to time at the far corner of the meadow, wondering if two hard black eyes glowered at him from the concealing trees. He felt better when Cappy returned home.

Cappy, to David's disappointment, could not give him any fascinating details or tell any remarkable stories about the man Blaze had treed.

"He makes a living by frightening ignorant people, and wearing a mask makes him seem strange, powerful," Cappy explained. "Well, today the tables were turned, he was frightened himself, so I guess there's no harm done."

"Why do they call him John the Baptist? That's from the Bible, isn't it?

"Yes. But it's a common enough Spanish name, Juan Bautista, and I'm sure his nickname doesn't come from scripture." Then Cappy smiled and for a moment searched his memory. *"And John was clothed with camel's hair, and with a girdle of skin about his loins; and he did eat locusts and wild honey."*

"Locusts? Ugh!"

"I don't know if *our* John eats locusts, but he certainly eats wild honey. He had trouble with the sheriff because he was smoking out bees in a dry month and might have burned the whole mountain. I suppose John's more than a little crazy, but he's harmless."

David, remembering the arm brandishing the knife and the horrible voice, did not believe John the Baptist was harmless at all, and he shivered a little.

Six

The next Sunday turned out to be a memorable day in David's life—a day no one in Spirit Canyon would ever forget—but at Rancho San Pascual that morning there were no portents of what was to take place.

Mrs. Littlefoot, when she served breakfast, wore her Sunday black silk dress enveloped by a big brown apron. She was unusually talkative as she leaned against the drainboard sipping coffee from a mug.

"The Woman has hired half the village to work at her party today," she said. "She hired my two nieces to wash dishes and my nephew Joey is being paid a fortune just to open and close the doors of people's cars for them. Imagine!"

"Hired your nephew?" Cappy frowned as he buttered a biscuit. "He'll slam a door on somebody's fingers."

Mrs. Littlefoot agreed. "Yesterday a truck from the city brought a load of fancy things to eat and a statue carved from a block of ice! What a notion!"

David marveled at how Mrs. Littlefoot knew everything. No one had called at Rancho San Pascual and he did not think she had left the house. Her knowledge seemed impossible. He suddenly imagined that she really had eyes in the back of her head and that they saw around corners, through walls.

She finished the breakfast dishes quickly, then tied her hat on with a long scarf of black silk and, still wearing her apron, went to the shed to wheel out her sturdy little motor scooter. She mounted it and put-putted off to Mass at the village church, her apron billowing, the ends of the scarf trailing in the wind.

"We won't work with Blaze today," said Cappy. "But this afternoon we'll take him on a walk down to the waterfall."

Something had been on David's mind. "Cappy, could Blaze learn to track? I mean like tracking down burglars by following their scent."

"I wish you wouldn't always think of Blaze doing only police or guard work," said Cappy. "Yes, he could do that. But I'd rather see him as a search-and-rescue dog saving people who were lost."

"Rescue, then. Could we teach him?"

"We could but we won't. If we spent a full hour every day just on tracking, it'd take about four months for Blaze to be a really good tracking dog. And you'll be back in school in San Francisco long before that." Cappy, seeing David's face, looked quickly down at his Sunday newspaper. A moment passed and without glancing up, he said, "Tell you what. Tomorrow we'll start playing a hide-and-seek game with you and Blaze. It isn't really training for tracking, but it's something like it. You know, some dogs don't need training. They track naturally, once they get the least idea of what you want."

David did not answer. "I'm going out to get Blaze," he said at last. "I want to talk to him."

"Fine, David." Cappy managed to suppress a sigh until David was gone.

Mrs. Littlefoot returned at noon and began cooking their meal. "Waiters in fancy uniforms have come from the city," she told Cappy. "Also, an orchestra. They have pitched tents all over the patio lawn like a tribe of Arapaho."

"Heap big doings." Cappy, pondering the final four blank squares of a crossword puzzle, paid no attention. When David came in to eat, he glanced covertly at the boy, relieved to see that the talk with Blaze had done David good, and Cappy remembered how often he himself had found consolation in telling his troubles to a sympathetic dog who listened quietly, offering no advice, no empty words, yet sensing his distress and sharing it. Even Xenia, full of the aches and complaints of old age, had managed to give him such understanding in the last year, staring up at him, great eyes full of gentleness and devotion, seeming to say, "I cannot help except to give you love—but that has no limit."

An hour later, when they started for the waterfall, David seemed cheerful. Once they were across the bridge, Cappy unsnapped the leash, rolled it, clipped it to his belt. "He needs some freedom to explore."

It was a beautiful day, bright with clear skies except for the distant banks of clouds lingering over the high peaks on the western horizon. A trout, a flash of silver, broke the surface of the stream beside them, then vanished in white foam. Blaze, forgetting dignity, plunged his muzzle into the water and splashed David's trousers as usual.

"We'll go just a little farther," said Cappy, standing on the bank. "Just to the edge of Mrs. Bradley's place, then go back home."

They were already quite close to Spirit Canyon Lodge, and David saw a long line of big, expensive cars parked just off the road. A moment later, as they walked on, he caught a faint sound of amplified music.

Cappy was just deciding that he should put Blaze on leash when David distracted him by exclaiming, "Look, Cappy! It's the little girls."

A trail branching from the road on their left led up a slope along Mrs. Bradley's stone wall. The two small Indian girls, dressed in their usual calico skirts and beribboned straw hats, were struggling to bring their flock of sheep down to the grassy bank of the stream. The sheep numbered more than half a hundred, and they were hefty merinos, plump and sturdy from a rich diet of summer grass. The movement of the flock to the stream was difficult because the heads of the sheep were almost as tall as the shepherdesses, and the girls could hardly see each other when the big rams moved between them. David was astonished that girls so small should be entrusted with large animals, not knowing that Indian children in the canyon learned to walk beside their mothers who were tending sheep and goats.

Since David had seen the flock only at a distance, he now ran ahead to get a closer look, Blaze following. At the moment the sheep reached the road Cappy unclipped the leash from his belt and was about to call Blaze back. But by then it was too late.

Blaze, like David, had seen sheep far away at the blurred limits of his vision, yet he was familiar with their scent—not just the aroma of their bodies, but with the special odor left by glands in their hooves, a scent spoor that enabled the sheep to find each other and to flock. The rich scent, even at a distance, never failed to stir a vague instinct in him, an ancestral memory implanted in his brain and blood.

And now, at the immediate sight and smell of the sheep, that formless instinct took shape, became a clear and powerful command, as though his forebears, the immemorial herders of Alpine meadows and Prussian plains, had barked a direct, unmistakable order to him. With a yelp Blaze charged ahead, pressing stragglers back into the flock, brushing aside one little girl who tripped over the long stick she carried. The girl shrieked in alarm, inciting the nearer sheep, who pressed hard against those ahead of them until suddenly the leaders stampeded, charging down the road. But in seconds it became a controlled stampede, banked on the left by the wall of Spirit Canyon Lodge and on the right by Blaze, who raced along the edge of the ovine torrent, barking fiercely but joyfully, euphoric in fulfilling his natural mission and utterly deaf to Cappy's shouted commands and David's yelling.

Blaze darted just ahead of the flock, and there he found open gates with grass, water, and shelter beyond. He had brought his flock home to the fold, and no veteran of the pampas could have wheeled his herd faster or more sharply than Blaze did now.

Barking with the satisfaction of work well done, Blaze turned the torrent, which was now a violent cascade, through the portals of Spirit Canyon Lodge to join Mrs. Bradley's patio cocktail party which now, unexpectedly, reached a poolside climax.

Marcella Bradley, although she told the story often enough later, never told it twice in the same way, because seldom in her life had so much happened so suddenly. At the moment of disaster she stood at a vantage point on a long porch where she had a full view of the melee.

One moment before panic erupted Mrs. Bradley lingered at the railing surveying the gala scene, counting her social coups. Below her the narrow green lawn framing the swimming pool teemed with guests sipping cocktails, nibbling hors d'oeuvres, while others prowled the sumptuous buffet table seeking more substantial fare. So crowded was the enclosed patio that waiters with trays of food and drink had to elbow through, but that was just as Mrs. Bradley had planned it, and now she congratulated herself on the number, wealth, and celebrity of her guests.

For today's fete she had bagged three members of the state legislature, a brace of judges, a family flock of exiled Iranian nobility, a lumber tycoon, and a mining magnate. These, plus eighty other persons of note, had made the journey to Spirit Canyon to enjoy her famous hospitality, and now she allowed herself to preen a little in self-congratulation. She enjoyed the role of Famous Hostess and regarded party giving as a competitive contact sport. So today she hovered serene and poised in a lacy party frock that seemed made of pink suds and bubbles, proudly viewing her arrangements.

Gay streamers radiating from a bamboo maypole wove a canopy for the five-man rock combo. Three silky pavilions, aflutter with pennons, provided shade for guests and their stakes served as mooring posts for extravagant bouquets of big balloons. A flunkey had just appeared with a box of skyrockets and Roman candles soon to be fired at the heavens. A gala afternoon, a lavish fete, thought Mrs. Bradley, confident that a certain society columnist would write those very words.

Carlos Jones was making his society debut as a singer and guitarist today, and he climbed upon a high stool, flexing his long fingers to limber them for performance, and several guests, startled by these knuckle crackings, cast him uneasy glances.

The leader of the band, resplendent in gold lamé, spoke into the microphone after a fanfare. "Ladies and gentlemen, we are honored—"

And then catastrophe struck.

A grayish tidal wave swept away the cocktail party, and Mrs. Bradley, gripped by a horrid fascination, stood paralyzed, gazing upon pandemonium beneath a crepe paper cloud. The guests, utterly routed by the avalanche of sheep yet hemmed in on all sides, had no retreat except to pile upon each other. The maypole whirled away, enmeshing five musicians in its web, as plastic plates sailed through the air like Frisbees, raining morsels of deviled egg, caviar, olives, *pâté de foie gras,* and herring in cream sauce upon the bedlam below.

Two portly dowagers, unlucky enough to be seated in deck chairs near the fountain of champagne punch, were all but drowned in brut while crushed ice cascaded over their coiffures and down their bosoms. Unfortunate guests lingering at the buffet table suddenly found themselves wallowing on top of it, grasping at quicksands of salads, helpless against the oil slick of gravy that gelled on their summer casuals.

Then the entire table was overthrown in the crush, collapsing at the same instant the portable folding bar folded and let loose a deluge of scotch, an eruption of soda.

Carlos Jones, high on his perch, was among the first casualties of the merino charge. Tumbling backward, he splashed into the swimming pool, taking the guitar and the stool with him, his salvation since they floated and he could not. Jones clung to these preservers with a death grip, fighting off bobbing heads around him, relinquishing the guitar only when its soundhole ceased to bubble and it sank to the bottom.

Around him the pool was awash not only with guests and floundering sheep, but with the entire flotsam of the party—hats, straw bags, napkins, a parasol, two canes, and a walking stick.

Nor was the ovine tide stemmed in the patio. Guests fled to the shelter of the house, leaving its double doors open, and the sheep pursued, routing the horde of Persian cats who hissed, spat, then ran up the draperies yowling.

Mrs. Bradley, standing as though turned to stone, gazed dumbly and unbelievingly at the devastation. She had lost all sense of time—had the surprise attack lasted minutes or an hour? With glazed eyes she observed persons and sheep being fished from the pool. Survivors cautiously poked their heads out from under the flattened pavilions. The din of baas, bleats, bellows, and shrieks had faded.

Most of the scene hardly registered on Marcella Bradley, but one detail impressed her powerfully. In the middle of the open gates, erect on his haunches and proud as a field marshall, sat a German Shepherd Dog. Lifting his head slightly, he inspected the conquered patio, then uttered one short but very positive bark of triumph.

It was then Marcella Bradley went into hysterics.

Seven

Supper at Rancho San Pascual that night was eaten in such silence that David almost jumped in his chair when Cappy said, quite mildly, "Pass the salt, please."

David did not know how he should feel, what was expected of him. It seemed only proper that they should all be mortified by Blaze's misbehavior, appalled at the destruction of Mrs. Bradley's cocktail party and the havoc wrought in her patio. But it was hard to be ashamed when he was secretly bursting with pride in Blaze's natural talent as a sheepherder. Twice he sighed audibly, recalling Blaze's magnificence as commander of the merinos, and he hoped these sighs were interpreted as sounds of remorse.

Besides being proud of Blaze, he thought the chaos at Spirit Canyon Lodge was probably the funniest thing he had ever seen in his life. He had had only one quick look before retreating, yet now, instead of worrying about the unknown but no doubt terrible consequences, he only wanted to burst into laughter, which seemed wrong, although he had a suspicion that Cappy and Mrs. Littlefoot, who avoided looking at each other, felt the same temptation.

Cappy finally spoke. "Anyway, she can't sue us. Our hides are saved by the gate and fence ordinance. This is grazing country—if Mrs. Bradley leaves a gate open, it's her own fault if sheep or cattle trespass. Thank the Lord we won't see her in court—it'll be bad enough just passing her on the road."

"My nephew heard people say that Blaze should be shot or poisoned," said Mrs. Littlefoot darkly.

"Yes, I heard that repeated. But I'm sure it didn't mean anything. Everybody was a little hysterical at the time." Cappy looked down at the coffee Mrs. Littlefoot was pouring for him. "You can hardly blame them. They had a few things to be hysterical about." The corners of Cappy's mouth twitched, then he forced his lips into a firm line. "Tomorrow, I'll call on Mrs. Bradley and offer my ... uh ... condolences, you might say."

Xenia, alerted by the aroma of coffee, presented herself for petting. She had been aware that something was wrong, of the strained atmosphere, and now she looked up at Cappy with a question in her cloudy eyes, her graying ears twitching. Then, straining her stiff old joints, she tried to climb into Cappy's lap, whining and complaining.

"All right, baby," he said, helping her up. "You haven't tried this in years. You know you're the world's oldest puppy?"

Again there was silence until Mrs. Littlefoot clicked her tongue and shook her head. "My niece said when the Woman went to lie down, she found a sheep under her bed and then another one in her sunken bathtub. Also, two cats on the living-room chandelier fought off all attempts to rescue them. And—"

Suddenly Mrs. Littlefoot could contain herself no longer. Her sense of dignity seldom permitted her to smile, let alone laugh, but now she burst into such uproarious laughter that she had to cling to the drainboard. "That Blaze is the devil's own dog!" she cried, pounding her thigh, almost doubled over. "Sheep in the bathtub, cats on the chandelier, people in the swimming pool!"

Then Cappy and David were laughing so hard the table shook, and both tried to talk at once, to describe what had happened, but both choked on their own laughter. Xenia barked in happy excitement, her tail waving in the air.

"A great day!" cried Mrs. Littlefoot. "A day that will never be forgotten in the canyon!" And, indeed, it never was.

Despite their laughter, Cappy did not feel easy until after he had talked with Mrs. Bradley the next morning. He returned to San Pascual greatly relieved. "She's a good sport," he said. "I never suspected she had much sense of humor, but she has. There won't be any grudges or hard feelings."

Mrs. Littlefoot nodded but looked grim, and David forgot all about Marcella Bradley because of the excitement of a new game they were learning.

It was to be hide-and-seek, with David hiding and Blaze searching him out, but they began not with hiding but with teaching Blaze to chase and retrieve a ball, a special ball made of rubber so hard that it resisted the powerful pressure of Blaze's jaws. Once Blaze grasped the idea of finding the ball, Cappy explained, they would gradually change the game to finding David, who would hide holding the ball.

"The command will be '*Blaze, find David,*' " Cappy said, and made a sweeping, circular gesture as a hand signal. "It's very hard for a dog to learn the name of a person, so we're using the ball to help him identify you."

David was absolutely certain Blaze knew his name, but did not argue.

The lessons were not easy, and in the next few days David learned patience above everything else. On Saturday Cappy began using one of David's sandals, having Blaze sniff it just before the search command and signal were given.

"Tracking," said David with satisfaction.

"Only in a way. To teach tracking properly we'd use a harness and a long lead and we'd set a course. It would be different—and much slower."

That afternoon Blaze found David unerringly three times—behind the shed, in the spring house, and under the bridge. "A few more lessons, and he'd be a real search-and-rescue dog," said David proudly.

"Umm." Cappy did not disillusion David by telling him that it took a year of training for a good German Shepherd—and they were almost the only breed used for such work—to become proficient and reliable in rescuing lost persons.

It had been a happy and quiet week; nothing unusual

happened until late Saturday night. At midnight David was asleep when Blaze suddenly awakened him with the sharp, serious barking that Cappy called a sentry's challenge. The shutters were open and moonlight streamed through the window where Blaze stood alert and decidedly on guard duty. Seeing that David was awake, Blaze stopped barking and waited, poised for action.

When a motor came to life on the road near the house, the dog barked again, and David hurried to the window just in time to see a vehicle—he thought it was Mrs. Bradley's jeep—pass the turnoff at Cappy's bridge and continue on toward Spirit Canyon Lodge and the village. Since Blaze, day or night, ignored the few cars and trucks that passed on the road across the stream, David decided that the jeep had stopped or perhaps stalled for a moment; that would be unusual, would arouse Blaze. But the jeep, if it really was the jeep, had vanished down the road, so David went back to bed and to sleep.

"It was funny," David told Cappy the next day. "I didn't realize it last night, but there weren't any headlights. No taillight, either."

"Not too unusual," Cappy said. "Some of the trucks and cars canyon people drive never have lights. In fact, they hardly have motors."

"If it was Mrs. Bradley, why would she be coming from the upper canyon? You said almost nobody lived there."

"Her driver takes that road as a shortcut to the city. It's very dangerous, a rock-slide area. But some people will risk their lives to save five minutes."

It was a warm, lazy Sunday, and David felt restless

knowing there was no possibility of an adventure such as they had had a week ago with the sheep. Late in the afternoon he took Blaze to the stream where he made another futile attempt to catch a fish.

Because the day was warm, Blaze felt less frisky than usual, and he lay contentedly beside David, now and then lifting his head to gaze into the boy's face with dark, quizzical eyes. Cappy often spoke of the love that existed between humans and dogs, a special love that dogs could not give or receive from their own kind. Now, as David reached out and touched Blaze's black and tawny coat, he felt a wash of this love, a deep yet undemanding companionship and understanding, a love without rivalry or question or limit. And their communication needed no words.

David rested his head against Blaze's back and studied the sky through the leafy strands of a willow tree, watching a circling hawk and a single cloud of pearl formed like a ship and drifting toward the white reef of the peaks in the upper valley. He felt love and security, he felt happiness, and he was puzzled that happiness should be such a quiet feeling.

A few minutes later he wound the line of his fishing pole and unbaited the hook. Blaze was investigating the nearby bushes and seemed to be chewing something—a root or a stick, David supposed, paying little attention.

"Home, Blaze. Home!" It was a new command, and David repeated it twice as they ambled toward the house.

Cappy was in the kennel kitchen, boiling a broth he would use to moisten meal, stirring a three-day supply in a big kettle. He turned when David and Blaze entered, started to say that dogs weren't allowed in this kitchen, then realized that the old rule did not much matter now that there was only one dog in the kennels instead of a dozen or more, not counting assortments of puppies. Blaze could be allowed liberties.

Kneeling, Cappy inspected Blaze's forepaws. "Nice dark nails," he said, "but they need trimming. Tomorrow you get a pedicure, Blaze old boy."

Earlier Cappy had been watching David and Blaze at the bank of the stream, marveling at how both the boy and the dog had changed and blossomed in less than a month. David was no longer pale and silent, no longer so withdrawn into the world of his imagination. In fact, when David was alone with Blaze he became downright talkative; Cappy often heard David outside his window chatting with Blaze so naturally that Cappy almost expected the dog to take up the conversation. No, Cappy thought, that wasn't right, Blaze *did* reply all the time in his own language. In finding each other the boy and the dog had each found himself, and Cappy felt a pride in his newly confident grandson he could not have imagined a few weeks ago.

Cappy looked into Blaze's face, scratching him lightly under the muzzle, and for an instant it seemed that the dog had read his mind and was agreeing with him, nodding his head in a very human way, pulling back the corners of his lips in an expression uncannily like a smile. It was comic, and Cappy chuckled, but at the same time he felt a little uneasy—the expression, the oddly human smile, struck him as unnatural and now, as he noticed a slight rigidity in Blaze's stance, a vague memory stirred in Cappy, a formless warning.

He put both hands firmly on Blaze, feeling the neck and the hard shoulder muscles. There seemed nothing wrong except the drawn smile, although Cappy was beginning to detect a peculiar cast in Blaze's eyes, an expression—and Cappy could hardly believe it—of fear. Yes, he decided, the dark eyes, for no apparent reason, were rolling and conveyed terrible alarm.

Then, under Cappy's touch, Blaze shuddered a bone-deep shudder that made his fur rise and riffle as though a powerful wind that only he could feel had swept through the room. He lifted his head, stretching the neck into a grotesque posture, an ugly parody of alertness, shoulders straining, front legs frozen. The splayed paws seemed pulled by invisible fingers.

Blaze cried out, an eerily human scream of terror and shock, a terrible plea ending in a sound of strangling that made Cappy's blood run cold. The stiff legs gave way and Blaze collapsed, lay sprawled on the linoleum, his whole body suddenly flaccid yet trembling.

Then Cappy recognized what he was seeing, yet for a moment the memories aroused by the dog's convulsion paralyzed him, left him unable to act. It could not be, he thought desperately, this was too terrible to happen!

"Blaze!" David was shouting. "Oh, Cappy, what's happened to him? What's wrong?"

"Be quiet!" Cappy recovered his senses, but his voice was a hoarse whisper. "Not a sound—do you understand?"

David nodded dumbly, but he understood only that a terrible thing was happening. He reached out to touch Blaze, to give love or comfort, but Cappy caught his wrist. "No, let him alone."

For a few seconds Blaze twitched and shivered, then, as though he had touched an electric wire, his whole body writhed, he rolled over on his back and his spine arched so sharply that only the top of his head and the tip of his backbone rested on the floor, his muscles drawn up in such a ghastly contortion that David pressed his fists against his mouth to keep from screaming while tears streamed down his face. Only moments before they had been frolicking on the path, and now this nightmare. It seemed unreal that an attack so terrible could strike so suddenly.

Blaze went limp again, but his eyes rolled wildly, and small spasms shook him like violent sobbing.

Cappy, now sure of himself, moved swiftly but quietly to the medicine cabinet, meanwhile speaking softly to David. "Go to the house and tell Mrs. Littlefoot to call Dr. Matson or Dr. Gomez in the city. If she can't reach them, any other vet should come. She knows which doctors, which numbers to call. Say it's an emergency—Blaze has been poisoned with some form of strychnine. Make sure Xenia doesn't go outside. And, David, don't run and don't let the screen door slam. No noise."

"Strychnine?" asked David faintly, not sure what the word meant.

"Yes. It's a poison usually used against rats. Now hurry on, David, we can't waste time."

Cappy did not say that for Blaze time had probably run

out already, and by the time any doctor came from the city it would be far too late. Strychnine! Even the name had a cruel sound. Blaze, he supposed, would die in the next half hour, and it was a heartbreaking waste of an innocent and beautiful life. Then, fighting off despair, Cappy gathered his determination and began to do what he could.

David stumbled on the sill of the kitchen door, hardly able to gasp out his message but Mrs. Littlefoot understood instantly and went to the telephone where she consulted a list of names and numbers thumbtacked to the old desk.

"Will a doctor come right away?" David's face, chalky, alarmed her. As she began to dial, she noticed his shoulders were trembling.

"Yes, one will come quickly," she answered, thinking that it was the end of a lovely summer afternoon, a fine Sunday when few people would stay home or at an office if they could be enjoying themselves outdoors. Even so, she nodded encouragement to David as she silently prayed for the help of San Pascual, protector of herds and herdsmen who had spoken with the angels when he was no older than David was now. Her face revealed no worry as she dialed number after number, reaching only answering services who promised to try to reach a doctor.

David watched her with growing terror, until she said, "Quickly now! Pump some rainwater from the cistern, put it on the stove and set it boiling. Then add salt and keep stirring it slowly. Put the oven on low heat in case we need to warm blankets or towels."

David rushed to these tasks, not suspecting what he did

was useless work invented by Mrs. Littlefoot to divert his mind and occupy his hands until this first panic abated. She knew how desperately he needed to feel he was helping Blaze, to think he could somehow fight for life against this invisible killer.

The water was boiling steadily when Mrs. Littlefoot put down the phone. "Go to your grandfather," she told David. "A doctor will come soon."

Just then another strange, unnatural cry of pain and helplessness echoed from the kennel, momentarily petrifying both of them. David threw his arms around Mrs. Littlefoot's waist and, burying his face in her apron, wept. For a moment she comforted him, stroking his dark head, but when he gasped, "Blaze is dying, he's dying!" she drew him gently away from her.

"You cannot know that," she said, her voice strong. "You are needed now to pray for Blaze and to help your grandfather. Go tell him the good news that a doctor will come, and do not bring on bad luck by believing in it!"

Because she could not find a handkerchief, she dried his pale cheeks with a corner of her apron. "Go to the kennel quietly. Any sharp sound or confusion can bring on another attack of the poison."

He turned back in the kitchen doorway. "Mrs. Littlefoot, have you seen other dogs that ate this? Swallowed strychnine?

"Of course. It was frightening, but they were better in a day or two."

She told this lie because she could not bear to speak the truth to him. Almost always those who swallowed strychnine died quickly, whether dogs or cats, rats or humans. They died before anyone knew what was wrong, what was happening.

As she watched David moving quietly toward the kennel, she remembered the terrible year long ago when a dog poisoner had lived in the village, a man whose sick mind compelled him to scatter pieces of meat made deadly with strychnine. All the cats that ate the meat died, every one of them, and so did all the small dogs. One large dog, part St. Bernard, lived because he ate very little of it. So many children had wept over their pets that year, and the killing of the unsuspecting animals only stopped when the sick man, for other reasons, was taken to an asylum.

Mrs. Littlefoot pushed these memories from her mind and went to the door of Cappy's room to quiet old Xenia, who was whining at being locked in. On returning to the kitchen, the picture of the beautiful dog, the last of his line, came again to her. She saw him standing in the dooryard, copper and ebony in the sun, and David, laughing, knelt beside him. Mrs. Littlefoot closed her eyes and her lips formed a hard line as she stood for a moment perfectly still in the middle of the kitchen.

No words came to her, she could not think of the right prayer. She went quickly to the cupboard under the sink and got out a pail and soap and a big brush with strong bristles. On her hands and knees she began scrubbing the floor inch by inch, not because it was dirty, but because this was the hardest work she could think of and work was the most powerful prayer she could offer up to the blessed child, Pascual.

The air in the kennel hung heavy with the chloroform Cappy had used to keep Blaze quiet, to try to stave off the deadly convulsions. David, sitting tense and quiet on a stool in the corner, fought off the waves of sickness the smell brought. The western windows were now tinted with crimson, the light of sunset deepening into night. From far away David heard a muffled roll of thunder, an approaching storm. Blaze appeared to shudder at the sound, and David clasped his hands together, his lips forming silent words. "Don't die, Blaze. Please, Blaze, don't die!"

Cappy, working quietly and with almost painful slowness on the floor near Blaze, swabbed up the last of the fluids and particles he had flushed from the dog's stomach. He tiptoed to the steel counter and examined what he had found—two morsels of meat, both of them studded with grains of poisoned wheat, lethal grains sold in stores everywhere as rat killers. So the worst Cappy had suspected was true. Blaze had not eaten one of the few deadly plants that sometimes grew in the canyon; he had been deliberately poisoned by someone who had taken pains to perform the terrible work effectively. A human killer—and Cappy was filled not so much with rage as with wonder that a thinking creature could perform such cruelty.

Cappy felt David's eyes upon him, questioning, and he gestured. Together they slipped outside, moved a little distance from the kennel.

Great clouds plunged across the sky, heaping upon one another, trying to smother the weak new moon. The thunder was still distant, but the wind brought a smell of rain. Across the yard the kitchen door stood open and Cappy saw Mrs. Littlefoot at her task, working by the yellow light of the lamp that hung above the table. He understood; he had seen such prayers before, and he was grateful to her.

"Blaze is dying," said David. His voice had taken on the lonely, withdrawn note Cappy had not heard for weeks. He put his arm around David's shoulders, realizing again how fragile the boy's body was, fragile and—tonight—defenseless.

"No, he's still alive, David. Every moment he lives counts now. It's more than an hour since the first seizure, and that's a good sign, a reason for hoping."

"Why did she do it?" David asked suddenly.

"What do you mean?"

"Mrs. Bradley. I saw her jeep on the road last night, and Blaze was chewing something down near the bridge. Cappy, how could she do such a thing just because of that party?"

"Don't say that, David, don't even think it. We can't blame anybody unless we're sure—and we don't know."

David was silent a moment, considering this. Then he said, "I'd better go back inside, Cappy. I don't want Blaze to be alone now. He wouldn't leave me alone, not ever."

David lay on a blanket not far from Blaze and a little later, when a clap of thunder brought on another convulsion, David buried his face in the cloth, covering his eyes and stopping his ears, unable to bear what was happening. But at last the storm moved on, rolling toward the peaks of the upper valley, sweeping the sky clean.

They watched into the night, each passing minute

158 / Robert Somerlott

seeming an eternity and each one filled with dread. Every stirring of the dog made them hold their breath in fear that another seizure was beginning.

Nearly three hours passed, and Blaze became so still that it seemed impossible his heart could be beating. He lay as though lifeless when they heard the motor of a car on the road and Cappy, realizing a veterinarian had probably arrived from the city, went out to meet the doctor. When Cappy had gone, David crept closer to Blaze, straining to catch any sign of life, and again David's lips formed silent words. "Breathe, Blaze! Blaze, don't leave me!"

Slowly, as if he heard the unspoken plea, Blaze's eyes opened, and weakly he lifted his head. He shuddered, but no convulsion came, and recognizing the hand resting on the floor near his muzzle, he touched the fingers softly with his tongue, kissing David before his eyes closed again in sleep.

In the kitchen Mrs. Littlefoot poured out the soapy water and put away the brush, her long prayer finished.

The young doctor stayed the night so he could examine Blaze thoroughly when there was no further danger of spasms. "The heartbeat's fine," he said. "No apparent damage. This fellow must be made of steel."

Not steel, David thought. Warm flesh and fur softer than anyone could imagine.

By order of the veterinarian Blaze spent most of the next three days confined in a crate Cappy removed from the van. The poison had passed from Blaze's body, but he needed long hours of rest to recover from the racking convulsions that had wrenched every muscle to the breaking point.

Since Xenia was too old to do any work, Cappy borrowed a hound from a friend in the village, and the hound, wearing a muzzle to protect it from any tempting but lethal tidbit, helped Cappy and David search the ground near both banks of the stream, combing the underbrush and grass for more poison and finding two lumps of deadly meat.

"What can we do?" David asked, anguished. "What if she comes back again with more poison?"

"David! I know you're talking about Mrs. Bradley and I want this to stop! We don't know who did this."

"Maybe a high fence," David went on. "With fine holes like screen so nothing could be pushed through them. Or maybe a wall."

Cappy shook his head. "There are some things you'd better learn right now about dog poisoners. No fence shorter than the Great Wall of China can stop them. Usually dog poisoners are sick people. Maybe they think they're acting because of revenge or fear or because a barking dog kept them awake all night. Oh, yes, they may have reasons. But their trouble goes deeper than that, and you can't guard against every possible attack by fences and walls."

"But we have to do something!"

"Yes, we'll do something. As soon as Blaze is strong enough, we'll teach him not to pick up strange food. Hard lessons—but there's no choice."

Yet even before Blaze regained his strength, Cappy took one step for his protection. He neatly lettered identical signs in English and Spanish and tacked them up in the post office and in the general store in the village.

WARNING!
Anyone caught carrying poisoned meat
near Rancho San Pascual will be forced
to eat what he carries!

A week later training began. Joey, Mrs. Littlefoot's fourteen-year-old nephew, arrived with his friend Sam Raindancer. Both rode tough little mountain ponies and wore fringed shirts and beaded hatbands. David thought they resembled the advance scouts of a war party, and he resolved to own such a pony one day.

Cappy cut a long switch, leaving a cluster of leaves at the thin end, then he explained what they were to do while he made marks on the ground to show where to stand, where to fall back when the time came. Cappy brought Blaze from the kennel, using an extra long leash.

Blaze, suspicious of strangers, gave a faint but threatening growl when he saw Joey, but relented a little when he caught scent of a bit of meat Joey carried in his left hand. Approaching, Joey offered the morsel, then dropped it on the ground and stepped back. The instant Blaze lowered his head to sniff the unexpected gift, Joey whacked Blaze across the muzzle with the switch he had held in his right hand and had concealed behind his back. At the same time Cappy jerked the leash, shouting, "No!"

Blaze gave a yelp of surprise, for the switch with its leaves was more startling than painful. When he tried to lunge for Joey, Cappy pulled him up short.

They repeated this at intervals six times that morning, Joey alternating with Sam Raindancer, and the last two times, when Blaze refused the bait, Cappy petted and praised the dog lavishly, rewarding him with a tiny piece of liver.

Joey and Sam returned several mornings, and sent friends to play the role of deceitful giver.

"This is the easy part," said Cappy. "We're teaching him not to accept bribes. It will be harder for him to learn he mustn't take gifts found on the ground with no stranger nearby."

Working in rubber gloves so his own scent would not cling to any object, Cappy baited small mousetraps with bits of meat. The springs of the traps were too weak to injure Blaze's nose, yet strong enough to deliver a sharp tweek, and the closing trap broke a little bag of quinine to give both the meat and the probing nose a bitter squirting. Cappy also cut slits in larger pieces of mutton and stuffed these pockets with the fieriest chili Mrs. Littlefoot could obtain. He closed the slits to hold in the odor, and hid these tongue-burning treats where Blaze was sure to find them.

Cappy and David planted bait along a marked course where they walked Blaze, jerking the leash sharply and shouting, "No! No!" whenever he lowered his head to pick up these discoveries.

"I think we're winning the battle," Cappy said one day

after Blaze passed three temptations without succumbing. "But we'll never be completely safe, David. Refusing food he finds goes against Blaze's nature, so the training's never certain. Well, I suppose just being alive means uncertainty."

Mrs. Littlefoot watched them work with silent approval, but she thought the private measures she herself used were far more effective. She removed the top and bottom of a tin coffee can, opened its seam with Cappy's wire cutters, then pounded it flat. On this surface she painted a picture of a dog with stiff legs pointing up in the air and a dark-haired boy beside him. In a lower corner Mrs. Littlefoot knelt with a bucket and brush; at the top hovered San Pascual, a radiant child, pointing one hand at the stricken animal and lifting the other to implore the help of heaven.

Mrs. Littlefoot had little skill in painting, so the figures were crude, the features drawn in with ink, and the saint's yellow halo had dripped onto his white garment. But Mrs. Littlefoot never thought of this because she knew San Pascual did not expect her to be an artist. The next Sunday she tacked her offering on a wall in the village church, selecting a spot near the altar of San Martin, the black saint, since there was no altar for San Pascual. Like herself, San Martin had scrubbed floors, so he would understand.

Mrs. Littlefoot dropped the tack hammer into her bag and stepped back to give her work a final inspection. She nodded slowly and with satisfaction. They were safe at last.

Eight

August came, the golden weeks of late summer in Spirit Canyon—hushed afternoons when even the aspens did not rustle and the circling hawk seemed to swim slowly against an invisible current through the heavy light. Autumn apples began their first green swelling, melons lay ripe in Cappy's garden, and Mrs. Littlefoot decorated the table with blue and white columbines. Blaze mastered close heeling in figure-eights and David caught a trout.

Under molten blue skies the sheep-cropped upper slope became tawny, then faded to the pale yellow of straw, while on the far peaks the snows retreated to the highest summits. A fire marshall, a big man in heavy boots, came to post warnings. He stayed to lunch, complaining about the lack of rain and the carelessness of campers with fires. After he had gone, Cappy stood gazing at the blackened foundations where the barn had stood, his face closed and unreadable. A carpet of dandelions that covered the charred earth there was aging from golden tufts to white puffballs. David knelt among them, making the last dandelion chains of the year to deck himself and Blaze.

In the middle of the month Cappy went away overnight to judge an obedience trial, and no dog he saw was as quick or as eager as Blaze. Competitive impulses he thought were dead suddenly stirred in him, but he banished such notions from his head. Meanwhile, Blaze perfected the response to the "long down" command, and David learned to make a two-note willow whistle.

August deepened, dragonflies hovered above still pools where the stream had withdrawn to its deepest bed; the nights became electric, uneasy with the flickering of heat lightning. The languishing tiger lilies died near the spring house, but a few sprinkles of rain were enough to make the Michelmas daisies burst to blossom. Cappy, seeing them, reminded himself it was time to hire Joey Littlefoot and Sam Raindancer to help him clear underbrush and cut wood for winter fireplaces. David had his first ride on Joey's pony, walking twice around the training ring with Joey leading, and Blaze followed behind, his eyes brimming with admiration.

David moved through the magical August days with a boy's heedlessness of time, oblivious of the final blossoming of summer, unaware that the blaze of August meant the first withering of the garden, the approach of fall. He lived joyfully in the present, thinking no further ahead than making plans for the next morning, the hide-and-seek game with Blaze, which now ranged to the farthest corners of the ranch. The past did not intrude upon him even when Cappy compelled him to write postcards to Aunt Nadine and Uncle Arthur.

There were so many things to think about! A forest in Blue Springs Canyon caught fire, thirty miles away, yet white ashes floated like snowflakes above the yard and garden. He dreamed of the carnival that was coming to the village and of the day when Cappy would let him enter Blaze in a real obedience trial. Two hundred points—he heard the judge announce the wonderful words—a perfect score!

Near the end of August Mrs. Littlefoot observed that David had grown. She stood him against the casing of the kitchen door, put a ruler flat on top of his head, and made a pencil mark on the woodwork. "A little taller than your father at the same age," she remarked, pointing to a line just below the new one. The casing had been painted since his father's time, but the old marks showed plainly. Cappy looked down at the line and the name "David." He took the pencil and made another mark high on the wall above the door. "Goliath," he said, and printed it.

With the passing days, Cappy felt a growing apprehension. The summer was ending, it was time for David to return to San Francisco, time to be ready for the start of school. He dreaded the boy's leaving, blamed himself for allowing his affections to be so deeply touched—a thing he had once sworn would never happen again. Yet he did not question the wisdom and rightness of David's departure. The boy belonged with Nadine and Arthur, the point had been settled long ago, and one did not go back on a settlement.

But the unbearable prospect was separating Blaze and David. Time would quickly lessen the dog's sense of loss, he would take comfort in familiar surroundings. But Cappy did not think it would be the same for David, who would be deprived of the one friend precious to him.

Cappy remembered the silent, distant boy hiding in the van and sighed, turning away quickly when Blaze and David romped past him.

The separation—and their separation seemed inevitable—would seem more bitter because it would be unnecessary. Arthur Wheeler's apartment was large, and a nearby park offered open space for running and play. Despite their size, German Shepherd Dogs made excellent pets in apartment houses because they were stable, not prone to howling, and unlike some breeds did not become unhappy when they could not roam. The problem, as Cappy saw it, was not the dog; it was Arthur and Nadine with their fears and prejudices.

If only they could see David and Blaze together, Cappy thought, if they could watch them play, realize how much the dog meant to David. The sight of the boy with the dog should melt a heart of flint, Cappy told himself.

He pondered the problem, reached a decision, and on the last day of August, a Sunday, called San Francisco when David was out playing, and found Arthur Wheeler at home.

"I think you and Nadine should come here to get David," Cappy told him, hiding his motive. "David would feel more assured, more wanted, if you were actually here."

"But that's impossible," said Arthur. "Nadine can't travel anywhere. The baby's expected the first week in October. David can travel alone. Just put him on the plane and I'll meet him in San Francisco. He's certainly old enough to manage by himself."

"If he can get on a plane alone," said Cappy with some

asperity, "he can also get off one, Arthur. There are two stops and a change between here and San Francisco. You can hardly expect me to guarantee the boy's arrival."

There was a pause. "You think he might run off?"

"Well, that's exactly what he did before."

This time the pause was even longer, and during it Cappy reminded himself that Arthur and Nadine had provided a very good home for David when they had no legal responsibility to do so.

"I'd scheduled a trip to Portland on Tuesday," said Arthur at last. "I'll cancel it and come and get David."

"That's the best thing! We'll meet you at the airport. You spend the night here at the ranch and return the next day. So it's all settled."

"Well, I suppose it's the safest thing. By the way, Cappy, I've been meaning to send you a check, and kept forgetting it." Arthur sounded less glib than usual. "So now I'll just bring it with me."

"A check?" Cappy asked, surprised. "Why? What for?"

"For David's room and board while he's been with you. The insurance company pays his living expenses, as you must remember. Of course, I'll have to deduct the money paid to the camp he never attended, then there'll be his plane fare and mine and—"

"Don't worry about it, Arthur! We'll see you Tuesday."

He hung up, pleased that Arthur had showed concern about David's safe arrival home, yet a little disturbed by the final turn their conversation had taken. Cappy had known that David had been left financially secure, but he had never thought of the substantial checks Arthur received for David every month. Nor until this moment had he considered how important this money might be to Arthur. At least, Cappy thought grimly, Arthur could not object that it would cost too much to feed Blaze. The money was David's, and there was quite enough of it.

But the main point was that Arthur would arrive Tuesday, he would see the boy and the dog together, and Cappy could not imagine that Blaze would fail to win Arthur's affection.

Cappy said nothing to David that evening or during the day on Monday. Twice he tried to introduce the subject, but his mouth went dry, and somehow the circumstances seemed wrong. Then, when he knew no more delay was possible, he steeled himself.

After supper they went to the porch. The week before Cappy had begun teaching David to recognize the more prominent stars and constellations.

"That's the Big Dipper and the Little Dipper." David pointed to them. "And the North Star—it isn't very bright but it's important in navigating."

"Right." For a moment they were silent, then Cappy forced himself to bring up the unwelcome subject. "I have good news, David. Your Uncle Arthur's arriving tomorrow."

"Tomorrow?" David seemed stunned. "For a visit?"

"Yes, for a short visit. He's coming to take you home. He and your Aunt Nadine have missed you very much, and now that summer's ending—"

"Home?" The boy still did not appear to understand. "He's coming to take me away?" David's hand suddenly rested on Blaze's shoulder.

"Well, school will be starting next week, I suppose, and—"

Suddenly David gave a muffled cry. He leaped to his feet and ran into the house, letting the screen door slam behind him, and raced through the kitchen and down the hall to his room.

Cappy sat quietly, filled with a sense of futility, blaming himself for not having prepared David better for this news. He had *told* David at the beginning that his stay in the canyon was only temporary. Why hadn't David understood? Yet he could not blame the boy. Cappy knew that he himself had been lulled into believing that this unexpected summer would never end, that they would go on forever through unchanging days in the golden light of August.

Cappy realized that Blaze was upset and confused by David's strange behavior, and he tried to comfort the dog, scratching him behind the ears and talking gently. But Cappy failed at that, too, and Blaze left him to find David's window and scratch at the shutters. Cappy heard them open to admit the dog, then close again quickly.

Cappy entered the kitchen where Mrs. Littlefoot, who had overheard everything, carefully hung up her damp dish towel and did not turn to look at him. He meant to go to David's room, to talk further with the boy, but in the hall he hesitated. The worst question, the terrible question, had not yet been asked. *What about Blaze?* Cappy had no answer, and suddenly anger welled in him. Let Arthur Wheeler tell David whatever must be told—it was not Cappy's decision; he could give David no false hope now, but neither could he deliver the blow of saying the dog must stay behind. Turning back, Cappy went to his own room, his step slower and heavier than it had been all summer.

In the morning David answered Mrs. Littlefoot's call through the closed door, but did not appear for breakfast. Cappy waited, and the minutes dragged by. At last he went to find David, who was fully dressed, sitting on the edge of his bed with Blaze lying watchfully on the rug.

"It's time to leave, time to go to the airport to meet your Uncle Arthur," Cappy said, making no attempt to inject false heartiness into his voice.

"You go. I don't want to." David's face was pale, but the small jaw had a firm set.

Cappy considered the situation. "All right," he said. "I won't force you to go, although I hoped you would, because I'm taking Blaze with me."

David looked up quickly, alarmed.

"I want your uncle to meet Blaze right away, to see how well behaved he is."

David nodded, looking away. "I don't want to go."

"Very well. But you're not to leave the property until we get back, and I'll expect you to show your uncle some good manners when he arrives."

Cappy left, taking Blaze with him, annoyed that he found this errand so depressing. After all, he was not going to meet an executioner but only David's uncle, whom he had invited to come.

After Cappy had gone, Mrs. Littlefoot tried to lure

David to the kitchen with a promise of apple pie, but he hardly answered her.

"I'm going into the village—to the store. Is there anything you'd like me to bring you?"

"Nothing."

A few minutes later her motor scooter coughed to life and she rode off, leaving David alone.

He sat silently on the bed, staring down at the rug, and minutes passed before he realized this was the first time since the beginning of summer that he had been in this room without Blaze. And tonight would be his last night at Rancho San Pascual. Until this second he had not quite comprehended the fact that he must leave, and at the same instant he understood why Cappy had taken Blaze to meet Uncle Arthur. Blaze was on trial, and David had little doubt about Uncle Arthur's decision.

He stood up then and went slowly to the kitchen, knowing vaguely what he must do. From a drawer he took the cloth bag with a drawstring Mrs. Littlefoot used when she gathered piñon nuts, and he packed it with the few things he would need—bread and cheese, matches, fish line and hook with his best lure. He would not need much—there were nuts and berries in the upper canyon. He would find a cave or a big hollow tree for shelter and stay only a few days or at most a week. Only until Uncle Arthur had gone back to San Francisco. Uncle Arthur, who so often described himself as a busy man, could hardly wait forever. David suddenly remembered the little boy who had come with the ailing puppy. David would find his house, he would live there for a while.

David packed one of the special whistles only dogs could hear, deciding to give it to the little boy to use in calling his puppy. He stuffed a pocket with dog biscuits as an extra offering, took a folder of forbidden matches for lighting campfires, and still without any plan—but feeling elated and a bit giddy—he crossed the bridge and for the first time turned left, hiking toward the faraway peaks.

Half an hour later he paused to drink from the stream, scooping up water that tasted like leaves. His sense of adventure had now pushed aside all other feelings. He momentarily forgot Uncle Arthur and was not really bothered that Blaze was not with him—Blaze would hear all about it later, David would tell him about the ploughed firebreak climbing the slope here, about this broad dark pool where the water seemed so strangely deep and richly flavored. Before going on, he examined the parched surface of the firebreak, noticing deep ruts and tiremarks. People must live near here, yet he saw no one, not even sheep or goats.

A moment later the stream veered away from the road and lost itself among thickets and boulders. David began to feel uneasy, trapped by the steep slope on one side of the road and by a forbidding line of briar bushes on the other. The sun was high, but the canyon so still that the buzzing of a locust in the dust at his feet sounded like an alarm. He had left the hunting ground of the familiar hawk at San Pascual, and here another hawk, far larger and fiercer looking, wheeled its own circle, claiming this sky.

David rounded a bend in the road, came upon a long straight stretch, then stopped in sudden alarm. He looked left and right, not knowing which way to run, where to hide. Ahead, some distance away but coming closer, was Sam Raindancer on his pony. Sam would certainly question him, probably force him to go back home. By the time they got there, Uncle Arthur would have arrived, ending all chance of escape.

David stood paralyzed, eyeing the thick briar bushes, afraid to plunge into them, and so concerned about Sam Raindancer that he did not hear a motor approaching behind him, heard nothing until the honk of a horn made him leap for the side of the road. Mrs. Bradley's jeep drew up beside him. She was alone, driving it, and now she leaned across the seat and opened the door.

"Need a ride, young fellow?" she asked.

He stared at her made-up doll's face, hating her, but not daring to shout that he would die before he rode with a woman who had tried to poison his dog.

"Hop in," she said, smiling. "What are you staring at? I won't bite you."

David suddenly found himself climbing into the jeep, impelled not by her invitation but by the sound of the trotting pony as Sam approached. The jeep offered refuge —Mrs. Bradley would appear to be taking David for a ride, and Sam was not likely to question this. As the vehicle started forward, David slumped down in the seat, hoping to escape detection when, a moment later, they passed Sam.

"Hello! Hello, Pony Boy!" Mrs. Bradley shouted out the window into the dust, and David now not only hated her, but was mortified to be seen with anybody who would call out such a silly greeting.

"You're Davy Holland, aren't you?"

"David." He forced out the correction, keeping his face turned away from her, wondering how soon he could escape without arousing suspicion.

"David, is it? Well, how formal we are! And where are you going, Master David Holland, if I may ask?"

David spoke the first words that came to mind. "Up near the Three Caves. I have a friend lives there. A little boy with a puppy that was sick, but now I think it's well. I'm going to see if it is. I'm taking it some biscuits."

Once he had started talking, he seemed unable to stop, and to prove his story, he pulled a brownish biscuit from his pocket. Mrs. Bradley wrinkled her nose, drawing it up exactly the way old Xenia did when she inspected food.

"How nice! That's a lovely thing for you to be doing— to call on a sick puppy."

"Not sick now," muttered David, embarrassed by her undeserved praise.

"They don't look at all like cat cookies," Mrs. Bradley remarked, and suddenly her face puckered. For a terrible moment David thought she was going to cry—a thing that in his experience grown-ups never did. "I will *not* think about that! I must not, I will not!"

David did not understand any of this, and looked away in confusion. Was she suffering guilt and remorse—as a dog poisoner should? It did not seem to be that.

"Well, I'm glad I found such a nice boy going on such a nice errand, David Holland." She sounded determinedly cheerful. "It makes me feel better on a morning when I'm so upset I shouldn't be driving alone to the city."

"The city? You're going the wrong way!" David exclaimed.

"No. I'm taking the shortcut through the upper canyon. I hope you know all the turnoffs, because I've never driven this road alone before."

David looked at her warily. She was taking a route Cappy said was dangerous, but that was no concern of David's. His only problem was how to get out of the jeep.

Mrs. Bradley, who had not been watching the road, kicked the brake pedal and they both tilted forward sharply. "Here—this is what I mean."

The road divided a few feet ahead of them, one branch climbing a shoulder of the mountain, the other plunging into a forest in a lower valley.

"Which way?" Mrs. Bradley smiled confidently. David gazed at the fork in the road, then looked up at Marcella Bradley's crazy sunhat, a big white thing with a jungle of artificial flowers.

"Which way?" she inquired again. "Since your grandfather lets you wander up here, I suppose you know the road?"

"Not the road to the city," David replied at last. "I'll get out here. I think my friend lives over there." He gestured toward the left fork. "Good-bye, Mrs. Bradley."

But the jeep was already in motion before he could open the door. "Don't be silly, David Holland. I'll drive you there. It won't take a moment."

David started to protest, but she rode over him, chattering about the unspoiled beauty of the upper canyon. When the road diverged again, David nodded vaguely to the left, while he frantically tried to devise a way of graceful escape. They were no longer on a real road, but followed a winding trail with deep ruts on the sides and high weeds in the center.

"What a sinister route!" she exclaimed happily. "But the dust and heat are terrible. Hand me a tissue from that box, dear."

I'm not your dear! he thought furiously, scowling as she dabbed perspiration from her forehead and wiped her bare shoulders above the ruffle of her yellow dress. Steering with one hand, she fished a spray can from a bag on the seat beside her, then squirted herself with a gray mist that smelled overpoweringly of lilacs.

A low branch brushed the windshield, sprang away, and matted foliage almost barricaded the trail, making it impossible to see more than a few yards ahead.

"Mrs. Bradley, you'd better turn back," said David, his voice unnaturally loud. He was suddenly quite frightened. "I don't think this is the right way. Maybe I made a mistake."

"Oh, dear! Well, I suppose we'll find a place to turn around in a minute."

But there was no such place. The trail twisted and wound, climbed, then dipped, but never widened enough to permit the jeep to turn around. Twigs broke off on both sides as the heavier branches were forced aside, and stripped leaves fell through the open window into David's lap. Since he could not see through the foliage overhead, the far peaks were hidden and he had lost all sense of direction.

Mrs. Bradley swerved, skirting a sudden outcropping of granite that loomed like a reef hidden in the forest. With no warning the trail ended, dropped off into a dry creek bed, and the jeep's front wheels plunged over the bank before Marcella Bradley could stop. She was thrown against the steering wheel, David hit a padded part of the dashboard, a hard bump. The front wheels spun helplessly in the sand of the creek, the rear were in the air, a foot off the ground. The jeep could go no farther.

Mrs. Bradley sat absolutely still for a moment, then she said, "Hand me another tissue, please, David. No, give me the whole box." She dabbed and sprayed, seeming unmindful that the motor was still running. David reached over and turned the key.

"Maybe you should set the hand brake," he advised cautiously.

"What? Oh, yes." But she did nothing. After a moment Mrs. Bradley managed a wan smile. "Does your friend live near here? Could we walk to his house and telephone the village garage?"

He was astonished she did not know that she herself and Cappy owned the only two telephones in Spirit Canyon.

"Your friend?" she repeated. "Where does he live?"

"I don't know, Mrs. Bradley."

"Oh, you don't know." She dabbed harder at her cheeks and forehead. David realized she had turned very pale. Just then a breeze rustled the aspen, and David straightened in his seat. "There's a house near here," he said.

"How do you know?"

"I can smell smoke," he said, and climbed from the jeep.

They found a path on the far side of the creek bed, a deer trail not easy to follow, and the going was made no easier by the thin, sharp heels on Mrs. Bradley's sandals. She would take a few strides with confidence, then suddenly wobble as she stepped in sand or deep pine needles. At such moments she stretched out her arms, hands flapping, and David thought she resembled a yellow and white bird whose feet were caught in a trap. The idea made him uneasy. He could no longer smell smoke, only the lilac scent of Mrs. Bradley, and he wished she had stayed at the jeep.

They struggled along a little farther, then David's heart sank as he almost bumped into a granite outcropping. They had walked in a circle, he decided, remembering that lost people did this. But beyond the rocks there was no jeep, they had not returned to the same place, just arrived at another that looked like it, and David wondered if there might be a hundred such rocks in the canyon, perhaps a thousand, all looking alike and none giving a clue to their whereabouts.

David, trying not to let branches snap back on Mrs. Bradley, looked over his shoulder and saw she was again fishing in the bag she wore over her shoulder. When she withdraw a package of cigarettes David said sharply, "No!"

"No what?" she asked, puzzled.

"You can't smoke here. It's against the fire laws and Cappy says only a fool would do it anyway." He had spoken without thinking, but now that the words were out, he was astonished and a little awed by their firmness. He had never spoken to a grown-up that way before. Mrs. Bradley, with a confused smile, put the cigarettes away.

"This way," he said, suddenly sure he would find the house and the fire he had smelled.

Then, just ahead, he saw the brighter, unbroken sunlight of a clearing, and the aroma of smoke became sharp, unmistakable. He had been right, they were safe.

David felt the sudden warmth of the sun as he moved from the shade into the open, and for a moment the brilliance blurred his vision. Yet he sensed instantly that something was wrong—the clearing seemed too small to be the site of a cabin, and the smoke was too diffused to come from a chimney. Then he saw the apparition, catching sight of it a moment before it saw him.

A phantom figure, a man swathed in cobwebs, stood a few yards away, his back to David. In one hand he held a burning brand of pitch pine, in the other a ragged length of cloth that he whirled in the air, dissipating smoke rising from the trunk of a hollow tree. Nearby was a bucket of water and several wet burlap bags. Then he realized that the strange gray shroud was made not of cobwebs but of old window curtains, torn and begrimed with smoke.

David stared, more puzzled than frightened now that the first shock was over. He could make nothing of this baffling scene until he heard the angry buzzing of bees, then he realized this was no ghost but simply a man smoking out wild bees to take their honey. The man was fanning the air so the smoke of his unlawful fire would be diffused and not attract attention from afar.

The figure turned, bending to reach for one of the burlap bags, and a long arm emerged from a rip in the netting. David saw a hand, almost skeletal, and danging from the wrist were ornaments of bones and feathers. He recognized John the Baptist the same instant John recognized him.

They stared at each other in astonishment, then the hermit, after peering toward the bushes to see if a dog was with David, took a menacing step forward, lifting high his torch. At that moment Mrs. Bradley pressed through branches and entered the clearing to see the grotesque, shrouded figure advancing on David. Lifting her head she uttered a blood-curdling scream, then snatched the spray can of lilac scent from her bag. She pointed it like a weapon, squirted a long stream, then screamed again.

Suddenly a cloud of maddened bees burst from the smoking tree. John the Baptist shrieked in panic, hurled the flaming pine brand in David's direction, then whirled to flee, crashing through underbrush that tore the netting. Long streamers ripped off to flutter from branches, while the man shouted curses as he struck and flailed at pursuing bees.

But David and Marcella Bradley, intent on their own flight, did not realize that John the Baptist was as terrified as they were. Clasping hands, they retreated blindly, David pulling his stumbling companion after him, running along a vague trail he supposed was the route they had followed before.

Meanwhile, the burning pitch pine John the Baptist had thrown at David seemed to splutter out. But one coal still smoldered near the bare roots of a thorn bush.

———

David and Mrs. Bradley ran on as best they could, branches scratching their hands and faces, tearing at their clothes. Mrs. Bradley's floppy hat was swept off as a pine branch raked her shoulder. Twice the strap of her bag became entangled, forcing them to halt while she freed herself. At last she decided to carry it in her hand, ready for use as a club if John the Baptist overtook them.

"Who was that horrible creature?" she gasped.

"His name is John. Cappy says he's crazy."

They stumbled ahead, Marcella Bradley bumping into a tree trunk when she looked back to see if they were being followed. Unnerved, she began to make little whimpering sounds of fright and confusion, noises so unnerving to David that he stopped and said, "Please stop crying, Mrs. Bradley."

"Crying?" She did not know she had made a sound.

"Yes. It doesn't help. We have to figure out how to get back to the road—or maybe find the stream and follow it."

"Oh, where are we?" she asked, leaning against a tree. "Aren't we almost back to the jeep?"

"I don't know." He thought they should have found it long ago, and he was bothered by the unfamiliar rocks. A mass of granite just ahead looked like a very fat man asleep on his back, a formation so odd that David felt sure he would have noticed it if they had passed this way before. He was not really afraid, yet the first cold doubts were creeping into his mind. He wanted to see Cappy, and Blaze, and Mrs. Littlefoot. All thoughts of his uncle and of running away had vanished.

"When we get back to the jeep, we'll keep blowing the

horn," Mrs. Bradley said. "Then someone's sure to find us."

She tried to smile, but there was a helpless note in her voice that worried David. She was the grown-up, she was supposed to be able to take charge, yet he felt she was counting on him to lead her, to decide which of these crisscrossing, almost invisible trails to follow. It was not fair, and besides, he hated her for trying to kill Blaze. He felt tempted to dart away, to disappear in the bushes and leave her to find her own way back—it would serve her right. But Cappy's face, hurt and disappointed, loomed in his mind. How could he tell Cappy of such behavior? David quickly reached out to steady Mrs. Bradley, whose left shoe had sunk in a gopher hole.

"This is terrible!" she cried, looking at her slender gold watch. "We've been wandering in this wilderness for two hours."

Two hours? Cappy would be home now, David thought, home and coming to find him. Maybe Cappy was already nearby.

"Hello!" he shouted.

"Oh, oh, oh!" echoed back eerily, and it seemed odd to David that there should be an echo in the middle of a forest, but a moment later he understood. The trees separated and on both the right and left loomed great cliffs of granite, dark towering walls forming a gigantic corridor. Here the trees were sparse, scrub growth, twisted and crippled, starved by the rocks.

"What a dreadful place," murmured Mrs. Bradley.

"Yes," said David. And somehow he managed to keep his voice from trembling.

The rattlesnake was six feet long and as thick as a strong man's arm. His mottled back, crosshatched with diamond designs, blended subtly into the rocks and patches of gray dirt, camouflaging him from both his prey and his enemies.

The rattlesnake had traveled far from his usual haunts in the foothills and felt uncomfortable this high in the canyon. He liked sandier soil, places that offered easy burrowing for the rabbits and gophers and mice that were his favorite diet. Also most summers the high canyons were wetter than he liked; like all reptiles he was sensitive to temperature—direct sunlight would kill him in a few hours; on the other hand, cold rain made him too slow and lethargic for successful hunting.

But this summer had been so unusually dry that he had slowly migrated into unfamiliar territory, and found this rocky stretch where he was gorging himself on unwary chipmunks and ground squirrels who passed this way seeking water from a nearby spring.

Today he had made a successful strike early in the morning, lashing out to bring down an unsuspecting rabbit, piercing the rabbit's soft back with a pair of two-inch fangs that shot a deadly poison into the victim's blood, killing it instantly, and providing a huge feast for the snake. Replete, he would not ordinarily have continued hunting today or tomorrow. But a few days before a signal had sounded inside him, a silent warning that soon the long sleep of winter would begin and he must store food in the fat of his body against the time of hibernation.

Obeying that signal, the snake today did not return to

his night-sleeping place in a crevass, but awaited the chance for a second meal. Yet the noonday heat made him languid; he lay uncoiled in the shade of a boulder, the long lethal fangs retracted and resting against the roof of his mouth. He had encountered almost no dangerous enemies in this part of the canyon. Only twice in the last days had he used the hard vibrators in his tail to warn off intruders. He had frightened off a deer whose sharp hooves looked menacing; and he had forced the cautious retreat of a bobcat, a fierce young female who had made a den for her two kittens not far away. His venom could, of course, kill the bobcat in one minute, but in dying she might do him painful damage, as one such cat had done him long ago.

Suddenly a strange, unnatural sound rang from the nearby cliffs, a two-note whistle, like the call of a bird and yet not a bird. Fast as the snap of a whip the snake's body coiled ready to strike and his fangs slipped down from the roof of his mouth into attacking position below his flat upper jaw.

Blending into the rock and lichens the snake waited, motionless and silent.

For Cappy Holland the return trip from the airport to San Pascual with Arthur Wheeler was a trying experience. Their meeting had gone wrong from the first moment.

Blaze, brushed until his coat seemed burnished, properly on leash and with ears at attention, had stood gallantly at Cappy's side, a model of canine beauty and deportment. But Arthur visibly blanched when he saw the dog, and nearly tripped over his own feet in his haste to get on the far side of Cappy so he would have a human shield between himself and this untrustworthy animal.

"Hello, hello!" he exclaimed and started to clap Cappy on the shoulder, but glanced at the dog and changed his mind. "Good to see you, Cappy," he finished uncertainly.

"Arthur!" Cappy returned the greeting, explained that David was waiting at the ranch, and then tried to introduce Blaze.

"He sure is big," said Arthur, approaching no closer. "I'll bet he eats ten pounds of meat a day! Well, where's your car?"

During the long trip to Spirit Canyon Cappy made attempts to explain David's devotion to Blaze, but realized he was having no success.

"Sounds like an unhealthy affection. The boy's just been alone too much," said Arthur complacently. "But now he'll have a little brother for a companion. Oh, it'll be different for David when Junior starts growing up."

"Junior?" Cappy inquired.

"Yes. Arthur Harlan Wheeler, Jr.," said Arthur proudly.

"What if the baby's a girl?"

"He won't be."

The conversation died, and Blaze in the rear of the van gave a sharp, disapproving bark. Arthur looked uneasily over his shoulder at the mesh-covered window.

When they arrived at San Pascual Cappy was not surprised to find that David had gone out. "He's playing somewhere," he told Arthur. "He'll be along as soon as he realizes Blaze is here. Remarkable how devoted they are!"

But Arthur did not hear this last remark because old Xenia, after inspecting the newcomer with a watery eye, growled her opinion, causing Arthur to move uneasily to the other side of the table.

In the yard Cappy shouted for David, then paused to greet Sam Raindancer who was splitting kindling near the spring house.

"Seen David, Sam?"

"Yes, sir. Maybe two hours ago when I was on my way to work here. He was going toward the upper canyon."

"The upper canyon?"

"That's right. He was with Mrs. Bradley—in her jeep. I waved to him, but he didn't notice me."

Baffled, Cappy returned to the house where Mrs. Littlefoot, looking worried, stopped him at the kitchen door. "There is a lot of cheese missing," she said in a low voice. "And I know what mouse has run off with it."

Fortunately Arthur had gone to the guest room to unpack his overnight bag and did not hear Cappy telephone Spirit Canyon Lodge, where the housekeeper told him that Mrs. Bradley had left that morning to keep an appointment in the city and, yes, she had driven toward the upper canyon.

"Where can I reach her in the city? This is an emergency."

A few minutes later Cappy held the noisy receiver away from his ear as an unknown person called Mr. Arnaldo berated him.

"No, Mrs. Bradley has *not* arrived. She's three quarters of an hour late and has utterly wrecked my schedule!

Don't think she won't be charged for it! You don't seem to understand that I have sets and shampoos lined up to the corner all day, and she solemnly promised, actually *vowed*, to be on time or early!"

"Thank you," said Cappy, hanging up.

He stood with one hand still on the telephone, trying hard to think calmly. One of his strengths had always been that he did not succumb to unreasoned alarm, but now for a moment he felt a sensation bordering on panic. Foolish, he told himself. He had no real grounds for fear.

Obviously David had run away. Perhaps he should have anticipated this, but it had seemed unlikely that David would leave without Blaze—which was why Blaze was now securely locked in his kennel. Despite this, the boy had fled and accepted a ride from Marcella Bradley, unlikely as this seemed. Mrs. Bradley's lateness at her hairdresser's salon probably meant nothing—no doubt such a woman was always late, everywhere.

But the upper canyon road, the so-called shortcut to the city! This was what he could not put from his mind as he paced between the telephone and the window. The whole upper canyon, to those who did not know it, was a treacherous wilderness. Avalanches thundered down its gray slopes, flash fires could turn its hundred cul-de-sacs into furnaces, but most dangerous of all was that the upper canyon was simply wilderness—ten thousand square miles of it stretching past the peaks into desert beyond. No one knew how many men and women—prospectors, homesteaders, hunters, and innocent picnickers had wandered until they found death in that hostile land.

Cappy glanced at his watch. Hardly ten minutes had

passed, but he telephoned the number in the city again. No, he was told, Mrs. Bradley had *still* not arrived.

Suddenly Cappy's patience snapped, he could no longer endure waiting. Striding across the kitchen, he told Mrs. Littlefoot to serve Arthur's lunch. "Say I've gone to fetch David—he's off somewhere with Mrs. Bradley, of all people!"

Cappy moved swiftly through the yard to the kennel and unlocked Blaze's run. "Come on, boy, we're taking another ride." The dog looked at him, then his gaze wandered toward the house, to the orchard and beyond the garden. He whined a question.

"That's right, Blaze. We're going where David is."

The floor of the great corridor between the cliffs was rougher than David had first supposed. Rocks were strewn everywhere; vines, thin but tough, seemed like trip wires; and patches of stunted underbrush, much of it wreathing dead tree trunks, lay in formidable tangles. Mrs. Bradley moved hesitantly beside him, smiling wanly when he nodded encouragement.

"You're walking much better," he told her. "You hardly wobble at all." She seemed grateful for his praise. Then, without warning, she staggered, pressing one hand to her forehead while the other clutched the air as though an invisible rope hung there to support her. David caught the outstretched hand, and slowly she recovered her balance.

"I'm afraid I was a little faint." Again she teetered precariously. "I'm on a diet, I haven't had a bite to eat since yesterday noon, so I suppose I'm giddy from hunger. Silly, isn't it? Well, I suppose I'm really losing weight!" She tried to laugh, but the sound she made was something else.

David reached into the bag that hung from his belt. "Here, have a piece of cheese."

She eyed the cheese ravenously. "I shouldn't, I'm absolutely off dairy products, and—" Her arm, seeming to have a will of its own, darted out and seized the tidbit. Without another word she wolfed it down, then silently accepted the slice of bread he gave her.

"I'm hungry, too." David remembered ruefully that he had refused breakfast. "We can eat over there—there's shade and no brush." He pointed to a huge boulder of mottled granite just ahead.

"Of course! A picnic." The thought of food seemed to restore her considerably.

As they moved toward the boulder, David took the bag from his belt and took stock of their provisions. Not much for two people, he thought, disconcerted by Mrs. Bradley's greedy gaze now focused on the cube of cheese and the three remaining slices of bread. He wished he had brought water.

A terrifying sound erupted at David's feet, a rasping alarm like the buzz of a thousand locusts. David stared down into the small beady eyes of the snake that lay coiled a yard away, and he was petrified. Rooted to the spot, he could only look at the horrible thing, seeing the deep pit of its snout, the curved white fangs and the little tongue darting between them. Again it buzzed its warning, ready to strike, and still he stood staring, mute and paralyzed.

Shrieking, Mrs. Bradley hurled her shoulder bag, wide of the mark, completely missing, but the reptile saw a gray and white shape hurtling downward, and the memory of his feared enemies the swooping eagles flashed through his small brain. The rattlesnake struck, its powerful body lashing out in a smooth, uncoiling thrust, the head veering at David's ankles to sink fangs into the leather, piercing the bag as though it were cotton.

David, awakened, hurled himself away, falling, rolling then struggling to his feet. Flight was his only thought, but from the corner of his eye he saw that the snake was already coiled again, ready to attack.

They ran from it, staggering and lurching over the rocks, Mrs. Bradley screaming when a startled chipmunk darted across her path. Bruised and panting, swallowing air in gulps, they reached a grove of aspens, and there Marcella Bradley collapsed, unable to run another stride, grateful to rest on green grass and moss near a tiny spring. For a few minutes neither could speak, then David said, "Thank you."

She nodded, still catching her breath.

"I lost the bread and cheese," he told her, suddenly humbled.

"I'm not hungry now anyway." She swallowed hard, cleared her throat, then tears began to stream down Marcella Bradley's cheeks. "This is the worst day of my life!"

David stared at her, despising himself because this woman, his enemy, had saved his life. Worse, he felt sorry for her now. She was not, as he had thought, a grown-up, but a child—a little younger than himself, although bigger. He had not suspected before that there were such people, but now he supposed there might be many of them. "It's terrible being lost," he said gently. "But we'll find our way."

"It's not just that! This terrible day started when I found Taffy and Fluffy, my kitties, dead! Poisoned! That man Jones must have done it. He threatened me yesterday when I fired him, told me I'd better watch my cats, but I didn't pay any attention, didn't believe he'd actually harm an innocent little animal. How could anybody do such a thing? Oh, it's wicked!"

David, watching her weep, knew she would not have hurt Blaze and he felt ashamed. Reaching out timidly to touch her hand, he said, "I'm sorry, Mrs. Bradley." Suddenly the Persian cats, creatures that had seemed vain and silly before, as vain and silly as the rich woman who owned them, were not jokes, nor was Mrs. Bradley, who now wept for the love of them, merely foolish. He understood her grief and shared it—a thing he had not known was possible.

"I understand, Mrs. Bradley."

Wiping away her tears, she looked at him, puzzled. "Yes," she said. "I think you do. Not many people understand—it's nice to find one who does."

They dipped water from the brown puddle at the spring, enough to wet their lips, but the water was too muddy to drink. David grew uneasy about their lingering. Perhaps the rattlesnake came here for water, and even if it did not, other creatures would—small animals to drink and larger predators to hunt those who sought water. Twice he had heard a strange stirring in the foliage, something moving that was larger than a rabbit or a chipmunk.

David had taken off his shoes to dip his feet in the water, and was retying them when Mrs. Bradley exclaimed, "Oh, look over there!" He looked where she pointed but saw nothing except the snarl of leaves, vines, and branches.

"I thought I saw a face," she said. "A cat's face, only bigger. But then, I've got cats on my mind today, naturally." She sniffed, but there were no more tears.

"We'd better go." But before they did, David found a broken branch thick enough to use as a weapon.

And so, both limping a little, they made their way slowly across the floor of the huge corridor, two tiny figures, hardly more than specks, dwarfed by the cliffs that towered above them.

Nine

Following David's morning route proved far easier than Cappy had feared. The canyon road, dirt with sparse gravel, told a clear story. The hoof marks of Sam Raindancer's pony were sharply stamped, disappearing for a few yards at a time where the surface was hard, then reappearing plainly. Only one vehicle, which had to have been Mrs. Bradley's jeep, had left recent tire marks in the soft dirt along the right shoulder. In several places David's small running shoes had imprinted the dust with corrugated tracks.

Cappy rounded a curve, came to a place where the jeep had pulled to the edge of the road and left deep tire patterns, the marks of stopping. David had left no apparent tracks, but Cappy suspected this was where David had accepted a ride, a suspicion confirmed a hundred yards later where tire marks veered right and hoof marks moved left, indicating that the pony and jeep had passed each other at this point.

Now Cappy drove more rapidly. The gravel had

thinned, the dust lay deeper; there could be no doubt of Mrs. Bradley's route.

"They went along here, Blaze," Cappy said. "They didn't stop, they passed this trail to the Raindancer ranch. See? Then they came to the fork and . . . oh, no!"

The jeep tracks went left instead of right, following an overgrown, washed-out road. Years ago a camera crew from Hollywood had filmed mountain scenery in the canyon, background footage; this trail, Cappy remembered, was one of the shallow roads they had cut to take in their equipment. It had been abandoned afterward and led nowhere except into deep wilderness.

Cappy drove down the disused road at a snail's pace. It was simple to follow the jeep now—it had left scars in disturbed leaves, in dust, in fallen pine needles. But taking the van farther into the forest was a risky venture, and after a half mile the route became impossible, the branches too low, the surface too pocked with holes and stones.

"We'd better follow on foot, Blaze," he told the dog, shutting off the ignition and dropping the keys into his pocket. He removed a small compass from the dashboard, clipped it to his watch strap. Blaze gave Cappy a thoughtful look, seeming to know that this was no ordinary excursion. He bounded to the ground as soon as Cappy opened the door, but showed no sign of running ahead or exploring.

"I don't think even a jeep could go much farther," said Cappy a few minutes later. Now they did not pause to look for tire marks; Cappy followed the broken twigs and stripped leaves, the deep scratches on bark. Through patchy openings in the foliage overhead, Cappy saw slate-colored clouds gathering. The whole atmosphere felt heavy, oppressive, and he quickened his stride, although he could not smell rain. Blaze seemed uneasy.

A large granite outcropping loomed ahead, and Cappy noticed that the jeep, swerving to circle it, had scattered a thick mound of dry pine needles and cones. The ground was sloping slightly downward, and he guessed, rightly, that they would soon find a dry watercourse.

Blaze, suddenly alert, moved ahead of Cappy, rounding the rock formation, then gave a summoning bark, and seconds later Cappy saw the immobilized jeep helplessly straddling the creek bank. He rushed forward, fearful that the passengers might be lying unconscious on the floor or in the front seat, but even before reaching the open doors he knew that David, at least, was not there, for Blaze sat calmly awaiting Cappy's next move.

"So she piled it up here," Cappy said. "And look at this!" From the floor he picked up a pocket comb. "David's. Must have fallen out of his pocket when the jeep hit the bank." Sniffing the comb, Blaze wagged his tail eagerly.

Clear tracks of two different sets of shoes led plainly across the dry sand of the creek. "Now why would they walk in that direction? David should know enough to walk downstream, downhill. Somewhere this creek has to find a river! But instead they followed this miserable deer trail. Why would they do that, Blaze?"

Then, before he had gone a dozen steps forward, Cappy learned the answer. "Smoke! The boy smelled this smoke and knew there had to be a cabin or a camp right over there!"

Cappy felt a surge of relief. David was safe, in a few minutes they would find him, thank God. But then, only a little farther along the tangled trail, Cappy's new confidence began to waver as he realized the smokey aroma pervading the air was not what it should have been. What were these campers burning? Aspen, pine, and cottonwood all in one campfire? And there was a smell of scorched herbs and vines. Slowly and with fear the truth dawned on Cappy—a ground fire lay ahead, a secret fire smoldering and creeping among the dead leaves and needles.

He tried to run, long, loping strides that were continually thwarted by branches and brush. Crooking his arm to protect his face, Cappy plunged through a thicket and, still running, burst into the clearing. At a glance he realized what was happening, a recognition that brought shock and almost sickening fright. On two sides the clearing had charred without flame, without sparks; he saw only thin curls of almost transparent smoke, and on the ground lay heaps of white ash that had been dead logs and heaps of leaves. Now the air hung absolutely still, nothing moved, nothing rustled, but with the least breath, the faintest murmur of a breeze, the surrounding acres would go up blazing like a gigantic torch.

He saw a half-empty bucket of water and rags someone had left behind and moved quickly toward it—a ridiculous drop to fight any fire that might burst up, but perhaps enough to wet his own clothes and Blaze's fur. In his haste, he did not watch the ground, and suddenly his right boot sank as a soft hill made by red ants gave way beneath his weight, sending him sprawling. He hit his head on the root of a dead stump, lay stunned for a few seconds, then Blaze was licking his face.

"I'm all right, old fellow," he said. "I should watch my step, shouldn't I?"

But he was not all right. The least pressure on his right knee brought unbearable pain; he tried to hop, but the sprained knee rebelled at supporting the weight of his upraised foot, and he collapsed on the ground again.

For a moment he sat perfectly still, head bowed. "There is a way," he said. "I have only to find it."

He tried shouting, but there was no reply, and he knew he could expect none. The fire had been smoldering a long time, anyone nearby would have become aware of the danger and gone for help. Folding his hands, forcing himself to think calmly, Cappy faced the facts. There was no hope that he could go on searching the wilderness for David and Marcella Bradley. Even without the injured knee he had no right to do so. His duty was to get back to the lower canyon and raise an alarm; this he must do first, the people of the canyon had to be warned.

But there was David—David lost somewhere in the wilderness to the west, David probably frightened and confused and in terrible danger when these embers burst into a raging fire, sweeping the canyon. This would happen soon, he knew it; and with this awareness of danger came a sense of how precious David was to him. Life without the boy seemed unimaginable.

"Blaze, come!" he commanded, forcing himself to stand for a moment. "Sit!" Cappy spread his hands in front of the dog's eyes as he did at home when they played hide-and-seek. Then he took David's comb from his shirt pocket and offered it to Blaze, gave him the scent.

"Blaze, find David!" he said, sweeping his arm in a great arc. The dog did not move. In the dark eyes Cappy saw a struggle to understand, a desperate wish to know and obey.

Cappy's knee throbbed, but he held himself upright as he had always stood during the game at home, and he tried once more, presenting the comb, gesturing, commanding in a voice that now was almost a shout. "Find David, Blaze! Find David—find him, Blaze."

Blaze hesitated, eyed the smoking ground, listened to the faint snap of burning. Slowly, slowly he moved toward the deer trail, head lowered, stepping cautiously as he skirted the gray coals that dotted the clearing. Then he turned back, paused with his eyes, dark and tragic, holding Cappy's. That look, full of obedience and farewell, spoke words Cappy would remember for the rest of his life.

"Find him, find him," Cappy gasped as the dog vanished into the thicket.

Then Cappy began crawling, dragging himself along with his hands and his left foot. How far back to the van, he wondered? Three miles? No, not even two. And he edged ahead a few more inches.

Blaze found easier footing and fresher air a hundred yards away. Hesitating, he lifted his head, letting one particular combination of scents register on his nostrils and in his brain, winnowing out many others. It was David's scent mixture he defined now; a dozen subtle aromas that blended together meant David. These touched a sensitive membrane that turned the scents into signals and commands. To Blaze David's scent was in some ways unchanging, a certain odor of his body, another of his hair, another of perspiration. Surrounding all these were larger, defining scents—human, male, a boy, not a man.

All these were heavy odors, and he did not confuse them with the lighter smells of hair oil and soap; those, too, were part of David, but he knew they were artificial and varying, not to be fully trusted. Today David had stuffed a pocket with dog biscuits, as he often did, but Blaze had not detected this part of David's scent until now, a quarter of a mile from the clearing.

Dry, the biscuits gave an aroma perceptible only a few feet away; but in running from John the Baptist, David had perspired, his pockets had become damp, and now the biscuits left a faint trail of scent particles.

Thousands upon thousands of scent particles hung unseen in the air around Blaze—they rested on the ground, on tree trunks; they were plastered to the leaves of trees David had brushed aside. Blaze could tell when David had run, when he had walked or paused, for David's own body in motion was the first disturber of the scent patterns. Running made them more diffused, the particles hung in long curving figures on the right and left; when David hesitated, the pattern was compact, and the difference was plain to Blaze.

Today the forest floor, shaded by leafy branches, had stayed cooler than the air above the trees, so the scent particles stayed low, they sank to hover near the ground and were not borne upward by rising currents of air. Blaze was working with his head low, although he did not really need to.

As he moved, Blaze weighed another sensation, the smell of upturned leaves and turf. Whenever a footfall disturbed the ground or its covering, a fresh scent was created: not the odor of the soles of the feet or of shoes—which Blaze understood in a different way—but a moister or a drier smell from the ground itself. The difference in freshness between these upturnings was so tiny that a man would have needed a sense of smell a thousand times as strong as any human possessed in order to tell which of two steps was older. But Blaze knew instantly, and it was this knowledge that kept him from backtracking. He could follow where his quarry went, instead of mistakenly seeking the place it had come from.

Blaze moved on carefully, disturbed by the powerful lilac scent left by Marcella Bradley; this was not a natural smell, so it made him wary. At the same time, other scent particles, clouds of them, distracted him; some animal had been hunting here since David had passed and had left a fresh, strong aroma. It was an animal Blaze had never seen but one that often left its spoor at San Pascual. He knew it was wild, a predator, but not like a cat. Another quality of the scent told him it often preyed on rabbits, but he could not guess its size or ferocity.

Then another smell came to him, a tempting aroma of

food, and he moved a few feet from the trail to investigate, quickly finding the morsel half hidden among leaves—mutton, raw and not a day old. Flies buzzed near it, advertising its presence. Blaze crept close, ears erect, nostrils twitching as he enjoyed the perfume. But at the same time he detected another scent, a faint, human smell—no person he knew well, yet the odor flickered at the edge of his recognition. This might mean danger, yet the human scent was hours old and the food lay there offering itself temptingly.

Blaze leaned forward, then froze, remembering the treacherous tidbits he had sniffed at San Pascual, the sharp burning of chili on his tongue and in his nostrils, the whacks on his nose. He turned away, refusing the lure, and as he did so the scent of the hunting animal came to him strongly—the marauder was approaching.

Blaze took cover, slipping into a clump of coyote bushes and flattening himself against the ground to watch. A moment later a sharp nose poked itself into the light of the trail, a head emerged from between two thorn bushes. Blaze, hardly breathing, studied the first fox he had seen. It moved leisurely toward the fascinating offering of mutton, and for a second the natural impulse to battle over food rose so powerfully in Blaze that he could hardly contain this wild urge.

The fox poked at the mutton with its pointed nose—then, suddenly, an alarming thing happened. There came a sharp, snapping sound and the fox gave a terrible cry as steel teeth clamped shut on a forepaw. After the first scream of pain, Blaze heard a bell jangling in the tree above the fox, and he saw the bell bouncing on a spring. The fox thrashed, struggling to tear itself free, and Blaze watched silently as it bit away its own fur and skin near the jaws of the trap, began to gnaw its own ankle bones. Blaze rose quietly and moved away.

Distracted, he had lost the scent. For a moment he stood confused, but instinct prompted him to move in a broad circle, going generally back the way he had come. He made his way among sharp rocks, through meshes of vines and over fallen timber. At last the scent came to him again, he found himself crossing it, and he almost leaped into the air barking for joy. But he satisfied himself by rolling on his back, wiggling his head, and pawing the air for a moment, letting himself become, briefly, a puppy once more. Then he trotted ahead, confident, the trail unmistakably marked with David and damp biscuits, with Marcella Bradley and sprayed lilac.

Then he slowed, moved cautiously again, warned by the vaguely human smell he had detected before near the mutton. Now it was very close, just to his left, and the odor of the fox, no longer a living aroma, mingled with the human male smell. He waited, fur bristling, but not making the least sound, and soon heard a violent shoving aside of branches and a human voice chanting words that were not like the words Blaze heard daily.

Ahead of Blaze, John the Baptist entered the trail and continued down it, the body of the fox slung over his shoulder and trailing down his back. There was blood on his shirt.

Blaze did not remember the day when he and David had

encountered this man, but he instantly recalled that this was an enemy. But now that Blaze was not on his home ground, he felt he had nothing to defend. So he waited quietly until John had vanished onto another path, then slowly continued his mission, pausing momentarily to test the air where the man had turned, and discovering that there was some sort of dwelling and many dead, decaying animals not far away.

The air along the trail remained heady with David's scent, and Blaze followed it happily, eager to join his friend. No breeze stirred, and the whole overcast sky seemed to bear down upon the canyon, cupping it like a great bell of dark glass. Blaze moved ahead rapidly, his front legs reaching out as though to dig into the earth, the powerful hip and thigh muscles propelling him along effortlessly. Movement was life and freedom, following David was love.

Then a vast hissing, a rushing, a roaring sound like an explosion, shook the leaves, and Blaze halted, turned back with his head lifted, every nerve tingling. The smoldering ground fire behind him had burst to flaming life, shooting upward, a fire storm exploding in the dry foliage above, a blast of heat that consumed ten acres of leaves, twigs, and small branches in one searing flash, leaving the heavier trunks, blackened, to stand like torches.

The sudden heat, terrible in intensity, split the bark of aspens and they appeared to burst from within while pitch pine bubbled and boiled. A huge cloud of heated air spiraled upward a mile into the clouds, causing flurries of wind to blow back and forth through the canyon. At

Blaze's feet a dust devil of pine needles fluttered upward to the lower branches of a great cottonwood.

A new and deep emotion stirred in Blaze. This was not a day like any other, not another game of finding David; and as he heard the distant roar of the fire, he ceased being a puppy. He did not cease being young, and he would always be playful, for that was his nature. But as he turned again to the trail, it was with a fixed and deliberate purpose that would remain with him until death. Before he had wanted to find David; now a realization of danger told him he *must* do it.

But the scent was fainter and mysteriously confused as he tried to move on, uncertain of the direction. Other scents, new particles, drifted across the trail and somewhere to his right a bed of wild mustard was releasing a hundred thousand spores into the air, emitting an acrid smell that overpowered David's traces. Baffled, the dog waited, tilting his head, looking left and right, listening, aware that the burning forest was advancing upon him and not knowing what to do.

Using his eyes, which he had hardly relied on until now, he found a bit of turned earth where Marcella Bradley's sharp heel had implanted itself, then been withdrawn. Blaze examined the spot closely. Unlike a bloodhound or a basset whose drooping ears could surround and cradle a scent, holding it in place, Blaze could not capture a smell. Yet it puzzled him that here, where odor should be strong, he sensed almost nothing. Then he detected a drifting of the scent, a drifting to the left that followed the wind currents toward a tangle of briars.

Head low, he plunged after the scent, briars clinging to

his coat, pulling at the hair as though to detain him. Thirty feet below the trail, David's scent and the scent of turned earth flowed into his nostrils as powerfully as ever, even though David had never trod this ground.

Blaze began anew, following another sort of track, one that did not cling to the trees or to ground David had actually touched, but a totally invisible track of scent particles floating in the air and descending to earth on a route not the same as David's but parallel to it.

Where Blaze moved now there was no physical path at all, not even the vaguest game trail, and he fought his way, tearing through underbrush, briars, and the low-branched spruce trees that barred his way. When the barriers were impassable, he gave up battling for each step and circled, recovering the trail at a farther point where it might be easier. And because of the circling, in the next hour Blaze traveled ten times the distance David had actually walked. The distance did not matter, the thorns and branches meant nothing; he would follow David and would allow nothing short of death to stop him, not even the fire, which was slowly gaining ground, advancing inexorably, while he was condemned over and over again to lose time by circling. Behind him he could hear its roar and the groans of twisting tree trunks, the crash of branches. Several times, when its vanguard flames were close, he looked back and saw that it was no longer an explosion but a widening gulf of flame that devoured all it touched. And a faint gust from a distant place brought him news that the fox, the man who had killed it, and the place where he lived with so many dead animals had all been incinerated.

Then at last he broke from the timber and was free in rocky, almost open country. Here the air currents had behaved differently, and he lost the scent, but found it again, picking up David's route farther to his left at a little distance from a huge outcropping of granite that now lay deep in the shadows of the late afternoon.

The rattlesnake, after its attack upon David and Mrs. Bradley, had retreated, hiding for a long time in a deep crack where the roots of a pine tree had forced the rocks apart. He would not have ventured out again that day, but the demanding hunger of autumn was again upon him. He had considered slipping to the waterhole to catch toads that lived secluded there. But these days the bobcat made the waterhole a risky spot. She was so savagely protective of her kittens, hidden in nearby rocks, that she might fall upon him if she caught him uncoiled. The bobcat would die, of course, but the snake did not care to endure even one paw slash.

So he had returned to his familiar rock and now, as the afternoon quickly faded, he was ready to leave, to take shelter for the night; his body was cooling, and this slowed him, made him sluggish. Uncoiling, he began to move, sliding in rippling loops and curves, but then stopped abruptly, winding himself into a taut coil as he felt the movements of a large animal approaching. Feeling the vibrations of its steps, he decided the newcomer was an unusually heavy coyote, not prey for him, but not a danger, either. Still, it was prudent to wait coiled between these two upthrusts of rock and see what happened.

The intruder came straight toward him, and he could

not at first determine much about the creature, since his eyes were highly efficient at close range, but of little use at distances. Then he recognized this animal as similar to others he had known in the years he had lived near the village. They were inquisitive creatures, potentially dangerous, and he had killed two almost as large as this one. Lifting the vibrators on his tail, he sounded a sharp, unmistakable warning. The creature stopped, retreated a little, then lowered its head, moving slightly as the eyes studied the snake. This, too, was familiar from the past. The snake buzzed another warning, lifting his head a little, and weaving enough to put any hostile lunge off balance. The fangs were fully extended and locked in place. Why didn't this animal retreat as all others did when given a chance? Why did it foolishly court death? And death, the snake knew, would be its fate in another minute.

Blaze hesitated, perplexed. Prudence warned him that this reptile was as lethal a creature as he had ever encountered and the only safe course was retreat. Yet retreat had difficulties. The passage between rocks that the snake guarded cried out David's presence. Crumbs of biscuits had fallen just ahead, cheese and bread that David had touched lay at Blaze's feet, and a whole pattern of scent perceptions connected with Marcella Bradley, who went everywhere David went, lingered on the ground. He had to go forward.

Blaze barked fiercely, a terrible threat to drive the long-fanged creature away, but it only buzzed defiance, lifting its evil head higher. Blaze crouched, ready to lunge in any direction, then the head came hurtling toward him, so close that the fangs brushed the tips of his chest hair, but Blaze had darted aside and back at the exact instant of the strike, and now moved back and forth a little farther away as the snake instantly drew its coils together again.

Now Blaze understood how it attacked, knew its speed and striking distance. He began to jump to the left, then to the right, snapping and feinting until the infuriated reptile lashed out once more. Its recoiling, which had seemed like lightning before, was a little slower this time, Blaze realized, and knowing this, he reared up on his hind legs as though to hurl himself onto the rattler, but instead, at the crucial instant, lunged to the left as the snake shot forward, trying to bury its fangs near the dog's heart, a strike that meant instant death. The rattler's head had not quite touched the ground when Blaze, attacking from the side, seized the snake just behind the head, crushing the base of the skull with a hundred pounds of pressure from his jaws. The reptile's long, muscular body whipped and lashed, the hard vibrators striking sharp but not piercing blows to Blaze's flank.

With a violent toss of his head, Blaze hurled the snake away, watched it writhe over the rocks, sliding down the slope, moving still, but these were the movements of death. The dog lay panting for a moment, then forced himself to rise and continue on his errand through the passage he had won.

Darkness came quickly, a black overcast night except to the east and north, where the sky was edged with crimson and yellow, flaring colors that were nothing like a sunset.

The moon was full and whenever the clouds parted briefly the whole long corridor of the canyon was illuminated. Blaze rested near the muddy spring. His coat was a tangle of brambles, his right forepaw swollen from a thorn he had just dislodged with his tongue. For half an hour he had lain here, working at the paw and recovering his strength. The fire seemed no nearer and he felt no heat, yet Blaze was not deceived. The wind told him that the flames were creeping along the ground—he smelled charring foxglove, which grew only close to the earth.

Animals that lived in the corridor were already in flight; a doe plunged into the clearing near the spring and leaped over Blaze as though he were a log. Chipmunks and rabbits darted past, and a complaining raccoon hurried on its way, ignoring the dog. Hundreds of birds, driven from their perching places, settled into branches above Blaze's head, filling the clearing with the noises of dawn.

Blaze rose, trotted a little way from the spring, then paused, undecided. New scents assailed his nostrils from every direction, the vast conglomeration of odors of roosting birds, animals in flight, and all the thousand smells of burning. Heat intensified ordinary scents until they became overpowering, just as an almost odorless head of cabbage sends out a penetrating aroma when dropped in boiling water.

Confused, Blaze began to circle, head high. Even with the moon shrouded behind clouds his night vision was keen, he could see anything moving, even small creatures like the tiny lizards darting over the rock formations just ahead. When he reached the boulders, Blaze poked his nose into crevasses and crannies, sniffing loudly, hoping to find any rock David had touched, any place where he might have leaned. But no familiar scent came to him.

He leaped to a shelf of rock a few feet above him, and slowly began to climb, hoping for a draft of air higher up, some current that would tell him where to go. As the wind veered, he caught a new odor, wild and feline, but then the scent faded, although it had seemed very close. Still higher he saw a notch between the rocks, a narrow opening where two heavy slabs of granite leaned against each other. Blaze stood on his hind legs, straining to reach it, to catch any scent that might be wafted from the other side of this natural pyramid he had climbed.

Yellow eyes suddenly blazed into his, only inches away, and a snarling, spitting face confronted him, the face of the bobcat whose den he had approached. Two kittens cowered behind her, and at this moment the bobcat, small compared to Blaze, had the courage of a tigress.

"Sccrrtt!" she screamed at him, slashing at his face with her claws. Hooked nails raked him near the left eye and along his muzzle. Wobbling, he fell back, losing his balance, and he rolled over the edge of the rock shelf, turning helplessly on the sharp stones until his body came to rest on the floor of the corridor.

The carved Swiss clock chimed two, but Cappy, sitting near the telephone with his injured leg propped on a stool, had no thought of sleep. His radio, turned low, crackled with reports and warnings each time the fire shifted or advanced. The conflagration was now devouring thirty thousand acres of the upper canyon, and Cappy marked each change on an ordnance map tacked to the table beside him. And each time he drew a new red line on the map he thought, "Is David in new danger?" Could, God forbid, he have wandered into the old Lodestone Mine section, now a square mile of inferno where nothing lived? Or had he gone toward the Three Caves, a neck of the canyon that might flame up at any minute, another death trap?

The lower canyon remained untouched by fire and seemed safe, but neighbors living farther away were injured, homeless, or missing.

A few minutes earlier Arthur Wheeler had staggered in, face flushed, hands blistered after managing half a shift as a fire fighter. He asked if there was news of David, then collapsed on the guest room bed, and now lay snoring, exhausted. The ranger who drove Arthur home, a friend of Cappy's, privately said that Arthur was "ready, willing, and completely unable." But he added that Arthur had tried hard to put on a good show.

Yes, thought Cappy, Arthur's pride would make him try. Yet it was not real pride Arthur felt, for pride was the value you put on yourself. Vanity was the value you sought from others, and vanity, Cappy decided, was the moving force of Arthur's life. He wanted to keep David not for love, not for the little profit that came to him, but merely to show that he was as successful a parent as he was a salesman.

Mrs. Littlefoot gave the ranger a jug of steaming coffee and he took it to his comrades who were struggling a few miles away. She then began packing two large baskets with food, towels, soap, and bandages for the temporary shelter in the village school. Cappy watched her for a moment, then said, "If the boy comes through all right, he's going to stay on here—to live with us."

She nodded, having known this for hours, and went on wrapping sandwiches. "You do not send back a miracle like something for a refund."

"Arthur and Nadine won't like it, but that's how it will be."

"They won't argue too much. Look now at who sleeps and at who sits watching."

"He's tired, he's not used to working. But you're right—he doesn't care deeply for anyone. Maybe that's his good luck, but I wouldn't want it."

She nodded. "You have done some things today, and still you are waiting. Is your bandage comfortable? Do you need anything before I go?"

"Just this." He handed her some money. "I know you'll stop at the church. Put my candle next to yours."

This had never happened before, but she concealed her surprise lest he feel embarrassed.

"And if it's appropriate, say a prayer for the dog as well. The way Blaze looked at me . . . I'm afraid for him. Very afraid."

After she had gone, Cappy moved his leg, decided he had improved, and that Dr. McKay had done a good job and was not a bad man even though he refused to accept dogs as patients, which indicated snobbery and ignorance. McKay, although rushed because of the emergency, had taken an extra moment to examine Cappy, listening to the heart and lungs, checking blood pressure.

"Pretty fair," said the doctor. "Pretty fair for a man who's just crawled two miles through brush, hopped another mile on an overgrown road, then drove a truck far enough to turn in a fire alarm—all with a disabled leg. I think you're in good enough shape to last the winter."

"Last the winter?" growled Cappy. "Tell me, McKay, how many dog handlers have you seen dead? Not one, I'll bet. But how many doctors?"

The doctor, chuckling, had gone; now Mrs. Littlefoot had left for the village and Arthur slept. Cappy sat alone, haunted by his fears for David, and at the same time trying to ponder the strange thing that had happened today. He recalled the crawl through brush and timber, the painful crossing of an anthill where the insects seemed tipped with acid; there had been moments when he thought he could not drag himself an inch farther. He remembered the grotesque struggle to back the van to the road and drive it, and after all that these desperate hours of waiting for news of David. It was no wonder he felt bone tired.

During the last year he had been through nothing that compared to the physical strain of today, yet often he had felt a deep, nagging tiredness. Tonight was different. Before he had been tired and old; now he was tired and young. Not many men could have done what he had done today; he felt he had won a prize, earned a medal, and it gave him hope and confidence. In testing his strength he had gained strength anew.

David *had* to come back safely—David and Blaze. They

had to come back because now was the time to begin life again, to rebuild, to look forward.

He took up the crutches that leaned against his chair and eased himself slowly across the room, out to the porch where he saw the yard silver and unreal in the brilliance of the moon. To the west the sky loomed black except for the tinges of red and yellow, the glow of the fire, the colors of death tonight.

He moved toward the drive, placing the tips of the crutches carefully, at moments resting on his good leg. At the ruined foundations of the old barn he hesitated, remembering that night when he had lost, he had thought, all that could ever matter to him—his career, his dogs—his family. Impossible then for him to accept that they were really gone! Sometimes he imagined their ghosts barking in the night, the happy barking of play. Ghost dogs frisked in the meadow, Donner and Blitzen, Inga and Heidi; and the last litter, the beautiful puppies that he had called—with dreadful irony, it turned out—his "fire litter." Ember and Flame, Sparkler and Torch . . . all gone, all ghost dogs except—perhaps—for Blaze.

Gone by fire. Cappy's fingers tightened on the handles of the crutches. Now David and Blaze were, if they were fortunate, wandering lost somewhere on that burning mountain. It could not, could not, happen to him twice this way. God himself, in destroying the whole world, had promised that the same agonies would not be endured a second time!

Cappy sat on the railing of the bridge and as his gaze wandered to the shadowed corral, he thought of a June morning, of David clinging to Blaze's leash, David hurt but unyielding, standing squarely in the spring house, his thin voice almost steady as he said, "Where can I find another collar?"

He thought of David and Blaze wandering through the July fields, playing tag where once another boy, another dog, had played. Blaze, tawny in the golden afternoons of August, and David saying, "Blaze isn't afraid of anything, Cappy. And Blaze loves me." Yes, Blaze loved him and was not afraid. Cappy also loved David, and now he, too, would not be afraid again.

Below the bridge the stream was rising, rushing in spate, and as Cappy looked down at the moonlit bank, he saw a twig first touched by the water, then tugged by foam and at last carried away. Somewhere in the west near the far peaks and beyond his vision rain was falling on the mountain, rain that would awaken the dry arroyos and creek beds, sending water flowing like a gift of life to the scorched land below. He remembered Miss Myrna and the night she had told him of the torrents that rise in the desert though no one can know from what fountains they come.

Cappy started toward the house. Passing the ruins, he told himself that the barn should have been rebuilt long ago. Yes, the barn to build, the kennels to be cleaned and refitted, the puppy room to be put in order . . . He would talk it all over with David next week. A boy could not be too young to learn about such things.

Cappy returned to his chair by the telephone and quietly waited.

David in the flickering light stared at a handful of dry dog biscuits. "I suppose if we wet them so they were soft, they might not taste too bad."

Mrs. Bradley coughed and rubbed her eyes. The wood smoke was bothering her more than she admitted, but at least it drove away all desire for a cigarette. "I'm sure those biscuits will be delicious," she agreed. "I don't know what made me feel I couldn't eat them before."

They had found a cave high on the canyon slope, had literally stumbled into it, for its mouth was hidden by bushes. David had almost reached exhaustion, and Marcella Bradley had declared she could not lift one foot after the other. Both had agreed to shelter here until morning.

The cave was large and clean; a little trickle of water dripped from its ceiling. They were sore of foot and weak from hunger, yet the worst thing had been the terrible gloom. Then David remembered the matches in his pocket, scraped together moss and dry twigs, and built a small fire near the entrance.

"You're supposed to set a circle of stones around the fire," Mrs. Bradley said, her expression far away.

"Is that right? How do you know, Mrs. Bradley?"

"I was a girl scout." Her face puckered but she did not weep again. "A century ago I was a girl scout—and I can't even find my way home!"

David softened the dog biscuits with water, and Mrs. Bradley ate one without tasting it. "Good!" She gulped. "May I have another, please? They're a little bit like liverwurst."

David left her and returned to the mouth of the cave

where he broke off the bushes so he could watch the slow
and terrible growth of the fiery arc to the east. An hour
went by and another. Mrs. Bradley dozed and so did
David, but each time his eyes opened, the fire had crept
closer and had widened. It was, he supposed, slowly cutting off their way home. Yet he did not think he could
run from it any longer. The fire seemed an inevitable force,
like an earthquake or an avalanche. He could summon no
resistance against it as he watched the yellow and crimson
flowing from the trees of the forest into the furze of the
great corridor they had crossed.

Now, he supposed, the flames were licking Mrs. Bradley's leather bag, and he hoped the snake was roasting. All
other creatures should escape, and he prayed they would.
But not the snake.

It saddened him to think that Cappy and Blaze had not
come for him. During the last hours he had believed at almost every minute they would appear to take him home.
He would have wept—but Mrs. Bradley was there and he
could not let her suspect that he was weak and frightened,
because she depended on him, and what would she do if
he did not seem strong?

Burying his head in his hands, stifling all sound, he let
the deep sobs shake his shoulders. Then a wisp of smoke,
not from their own fire, drifted past him. Soon the smoke
would billow up the slope, would reach his feet, great
clouds to fill the cave, to fill the canyon, white clouds.
Breathing a little of the smoke, he thought of whiteness,
of lying down in the cave and letting the soft whiteness
envelop him, cover him like the vast banks of unending
snow

But something hard in his pocket pressed against his leg, and he took out the steel whistle that only dogs could hear, the whistle he had chosen as a gift for the little boy with the puppy. That was a lifetime ago. Putting the whistle to his lips, he blew a short and a long blast, a short and a long—the signal he used to call Blaze from afar at San Pascual.

Closing his eyes, he nodded, the smoke making him sleepy. He drifted into a dream, knowing he must soon rouse himself because Mrs. Bradley needed him. But for a moment he was hiding in the cool shadows beneath the bridge, the water flowed gently over his bare feet, soothing him. Nearby Blaze searched for him, hide-and-seek, but he made no sound. Then Blaze, with a jubilant bark, found him, licking his face and hands, kissing him.

David, awakening, slumped backward onto the floor of the cave and looked upward into Blaze's face. Blood had dried on the dog's muzzle, the flesh was raw and angry near the left eye, and when David reached up to touch Blaze's chest, to make sure he was real, his hands touched more dry blood and knots of brambles.

"Blaze! You came for me, Blaze!" His heart swelled until it seemed to be breaking.

Cowering in the back of the cave, Marcella Bradley thought she saw a huge wolf enter and begin to devour David Holland. She clapped her hands against her mouth, too terrified to scream.

Blaze led them carefully down the slope, skirting the edge of the fire, and when the woman hung back or seemed too tired to go on, he went to her and nudged her gently with his nose as he would have encouraged a lagging sheep, and once when she tried to sit on the ground, he growled and would not permit her to linger.

"I think the dog's lost," Mrs. Bradley moaned.

"No," David told her. "He can follow the scent home. It's called backtracking. Please don't worry, Mrs. Bradley. Blaze knows all about backtracking."

But even as he reassured her, David's own confidence suffered a jolt. A fine, thin rain began to fall, enough to dampen the land, but certainly nothing to discourage the roaring fire on their left. Indeed, above the fire the rain turned to clouds of white steam before it ever touched the flaming treetops.

But would the rain wash away the trail Blaze was following? David felt deeply afraid it would, for it seemed impossible that Blaze could detect scent through the moisture now covering the ground. Soon they would be lost again, and his spirits sank.

Blaze, limping but still hurrying his charges along, felt his strength returning with the new coolness, and the moisture held the scent particles to the ground and glued them to the surfaces of the rocks, the bark of the stunted trees. To him, the damp night, like a dewy morning, told the clearest stories of all, and as he moved now he read the movements of animals and birds, knew much about the least creature that had passed this way in flight.

But he was not, as David believed, backtracking. The old route lay engulfed in fire; of the thousands of trees they had passed that day not one now stood except as a blazing or blackened stump. They could not pass through this furnace, so Blaze now led them along another route, urging them down a vague path that would bring them to water, to the canyon stream that marked the way to San Pascual.

They walked through the night and into the dawn. Eventually they found themselves no longer alone in the canyon. Above them helicopters hovered in the pale sky, and parachutes blossomed as fire fighters were dropped into the wilderness like invading troops behind enemy lines, men who would battle the conflagration from the rear, cutting breaks, setting back fires.

When they reached the lower canyon road it was crowded with men driving mules laden with equipment, axes and shovels, and drums of chemicals. Between the road and the stream lay rangers who slept where they had finally lain down to take an hour's rest before returning to the struggle.

Weary though they were, neither David nor Marcella Bradley thought of asking these men to help them reach home. With Blaze, they had come this far on their own, emerging from the very heart of the burning canyon, and now they would finish the last two miles alone. They limped, they were bedraggled and soot blackened, their clothes were torn, they were half blinded from smoke—yet they walked proudly. They had done something.

They paused at the top of a little rise and David gazed down on Rancho San Pascual. The windmill turned peacefully, the house with its stone chimney looked strong and secure; it was even more beautiful than it had seemed to David on that day when he first saw it, a summer ago, a lifetime ago, when he was a child.

At the cattle guard, Mrs. Bradley, numb and staring straight ahead but with her chin high, allowed David to take her arm in case she should stumble. He cupped her elbow, and they moved ahead, their slowness and stiffness lending them an odd elegance, a tall woman and her tiny escort entering a ballroom.

Raising his head, Blaze barked to proclaim their return, telling old Xenia and Mrs. Littlefoot, telling Cappy who sat by the telephone, his head in his hands, and telling the canine ghosts that played forever in the meadows of San Pascual that he had brought his charges home, that he had not failed them.